A DAUGHTER'S DESPERATION

Victorian Romance

FAYE GODWIN

Tica House Publishing

Sweet Romance that Delights and Enchants!

Copyright © 2019 by Faye Godwin

All rights reserved.

No part of this book may be reproduced in any form or by any electronic or mechanical means, including information storage and retrieval systems, without written permission from the author, except for the use of brief quotations in a book review.

PERSONAL WORD FROM THE AUTHOR

Dearest Readers,

I'm so delighted that you have chosen one of my books to read. I am proud to be a part of the team of writers at Tica House Publishing. Our goal is to inspire, entertain, and give you many hours of reading pleasure. Your kind words and loving readership are deeply appreciated.

I would like to personally invite you to sign up for updates and to become part of our **Exclusive Reader Club**—it's completely Free to Join! I'd love to welcome you!

Much love,

Faye Godwin

FAYE GODWIN

VISIT HERE to Join our Reader's Club and to Receive Tica House Updates;

https://victorian.subscribemenow.com/

PART I

CHAPTER 1

The sounds of the marketplace were so loud that Elsie could barely hear the vendor at the bakery stall. She leaned in a little closer, trying to concentrate as well as she could, but the noise around her was chaotic and distracting. Voices of all kinds haggled and shouted and laughed, children's footsteps slapped on the cobblestones, hoofbeats and squeaking carriage wheels traveled down the road, and dogs barked—even chickens squawked at one market stall. This place was a marvel, one of the rare spots near Elsie's slum where farmers could still set up stands in order to sell their wares cheaply.

"Sixpence?" Elsie asked, looking up at the baker as he loomed over her.

"To you, yes." He looked her up and down, with a sneer crinkling his lip.

Elsie was suddenly acutely aware of her dirty dress and scuffed shoes. She leaned forward a tiny bit, hoping that the ragged hem of her dress would hide the fact that her socks were mismatched and riddled with holes. Mother had told her to negotiate, and she tried to be brave as she stared up at the baker's mean eyes.

"Four pennies," she said, swallowing. "And not a farthing more."

The baker snorted, stepping back. "Don't waste my time," he spat. "Get out of my sight."

"No – please, please." Elsie stepped forward, almost dropping the coins she had clutched in her hand. "Please, it's all right. I-I have the money right here."

The baker moved back, still sneering at her. Elsie scraped together all the courage she could find, thinking of how far the money in her hand had to stretch.

"Five pence," she croaked, trying not to sound as terrified as she was.

The baker studied her for a few seconds, then shrugged. "Very well."

He watched Elsie slowly count the coins onto the front of his market stall, and only after he had carefully inspected each coin did he turn to the baskets of bread behind him. Elsie could feel her mouth water as the baker looked through the loaves of yesterday's bread in the baskets, finally selecting the smallest one before he turned back to her and slapped it carelessly onto the counter.

"Thank you," Elsie said. She grabbed the bread in both hands; it felt real and solid, and she couldn't wait to feel its reassuring weight in her stomach. She brought it close to her face and took a deep breath. It was a little stale, but to her starving senses, it still smelled wonderful.

"Push off," snapped the baker. "You're chasing away customers with your dirty face."

Obediently, Elsie turned and scampered away. She could still feel the weight of a single penny in her pocket, and this loaf would feed her and her mother for a few days. Gratitude filled her heart. Sometimes, at least, Philip could still be fairly decent – and giving them sixpence yesterday had been one of those times.

Elsie moved through the marketplace, heading back toward the slums. She lingered for a moment at each stall, gazing up at the different wares, dreaming of a different world where she could afford some of the things she saw for sale. There were gorgeous, round fruits, gleaming with color, looking so juicy that Elsie could almost taste their sweetness as she stared at them: apples and peaches, plums and beautiful plump pears. The next stall had vegetables, and Elsie's stomach rumbled again as she looked at the array. She couldn't remember the last time she'd bitten into a crunchy carrot.

Sometimes Mama would toss a slightly wilted turnip into the soup, but that was about all.

Giving up on staring at the food stalls, Elsie looked around at the people instead. While she could see a few grubby-faced urchins who looked similar to her, she noticed some women in neat clothing, carefully inspecting the stallholders' wares. Nobody tried to chase these women off – instead, stallholders nodded in deference to them, showing off their best products, hoping to fetch good prices. Mama had told her once that these people were housekeepers or cooks for some of the fancy houses on the other side of town.

Elsie gave a little sigh as she left the marketplace and headed down the streets, the landscape changing around her the further she walked. Sometimes, she was so jealous of those housekeepers. She wondered what it was like to buy anything you liked to eat – to be able to have meat and potatoes with every meal. But Mama told her that it didn't do any good to complain or be envious of people. So instead, Elsie lifted her eyes and quickened her step, wanting to get home as soon as she could.

The smell of the slum hit her before she could see it. Cobblestones under her feet gave way to dirt and mud as the stench of disease and decay rose all around her. There were puddles in the streets, each with a shiny, oily shimmer on the top. Horse manure lay old and stale among the puddles, and there was the carcass of a dead rat in the street, its ugly yellow teeth dry and pale in the sun. Elsie tried not to look at it, skirting around a pile of nameless rubbish and turning down a side street.

Here, the houses were built humble-jumble around her, leaning on one another like the drunken old men that sometimes staggered down the street from the direction of the pub. More often than not, they fell down in the streets and snored there until morning came and someone robbed them before chasing them off. There was no grass here, no fountains or trees, and no gardens. Just dirty walls rising all around Elsie, broken window-panes glaring like gaps between teeth, doors half hanging off their hinges. She tried not to look at any of the people walking on the street around her. Some of them had frightening eyes, and others were so thin and pale she feared they might drop dead right in front of her.

At last, she was home. She rapped gently on the door, watching as paint flaked from its weather-beaten surface.

"It's me," she called out. "Elsie Griggs."

Stepping inside, she passed two doors on either side of the dark hall before turning right into their own.

The tenement was bare and gray. Elsie tried not to look at the dirty walls, the insidious bloom of black mold in one corner, or the glimpses of daylight she could see through the holes around the single window. Its pale, washed-out light felt secondhand and diluted as it spilled over the rest of the room —over the lousy sleeping mats on the floor, the fireplace with its single, grayish coal huddling, lonely, at its center. And

Mama, sitting on her sleeping mat, trying to darn one of Philip's socks.

"Elsie." Mama smiled, her expression lifting the wrinkles around her eyes, making her look just a little younger. "I'm so glad you're home safe. I do worry about you."

"I'm fine, Mama." Elsie slipped her shopping basket off her arm and set it down on the single table in the corner. The table wobbled precariously, its loose leg squeaking. "I've brought us a whole loaf of bread. There was even a penny left for some coal for the fire."

"You're a good girl, Elsie," said Mama. "Thank you."

"Where's Philip?" Elsie asked. "In the bathroom?"

Mama glanced through their open door to the narrow hallway outside their room which lead to the dirty bathroom at the end.

"No," she said, and her voice was thick with worry. "I haven't seen him all day."

Elsie jumped up to close the door before being told to do so. Mama had warned her many times to keep it closed. She scurried back and sighed as she cut two fat slices of bread and put them down on their tin plates. She carried the plates over to her mother and sat down beside her, giving her one.

"I wish Philip would come home," she murmured.

Mama broke off a chunk of the bread and nibbled on it. Her

bites were small and quick, trying not to look as desperately hungry as Elsie knew she was. "Me too, my dear," she said.

"Where do you think he is this time?"

Mama looked away. Elsie knew she didn't really want to answer. "I don't know," she finally said reluctantly. "All I know is that we have to pray for him. Maybe the good Lord can control that boy – because I certainly can't."

Her words frightened Elsie. "Do you think he's safe?"

Mama gave her a kindly look, putting a hand on her shoulder. "I hope so," she said. "I truly hope so. It was good of him to bring us that money." She smiled, taking another bite of the bread.

"It was," Elsie agreed. "I just hope he brings us more again soon."

"I don't know what to hope," said Mama softly. "Except that he's earning this money by honest means."

"I don't understand." Elsie's eyes widened. "Do you think he's *stealing*, Mama? They'll hang him!"

"Hush, child." Mama put a hand on her arm. "Don't you worry about it. Your brother is brighter than that." But her voice sounded doubtful.

"Maybe he has a job," said Elsie, trying not to imagine her brother as a thief. "Maybe he just won't tell us because he's angry about Papa."

"Let's not talk about your papa, my dear." Mama smiled, squeezing Elsie's arm. "He's gone now, and you already have too much to worry about." She sighed. "You're only twelve years old. Just a little girl. I hate to think…" She looked away, her hand falling to her side.

Elsie could sense her mother's dismay and immediately regretted mentioning her father. "It's all right," she said. "Look, this bread will last us days. And then I'll go and ask Mrs. Patterson if she has any mending for us. We'll be all right for the rent on Monday. I know we will be."

Mama smiled at her. "You're such a good girl, Elsie," she said again. "And when it comes to money, I have some good news."

"You do?"

"Yes." Her smile grew a little strained. "Although it might be a little difficult at first…" She paused.

"What is it? Tell me. Is it a job for me?"

"Yes," said Mama. "There's a position open that I think you might suit perfectly."

Elsie sat up straight. "Where?"

"At the Whiston Manor – it's a beautiful estate on the other side of London. Old Agnes Whiston lives there. She's a very rich widow, but she's getting old now, and she needs a personal maid. She has plenty of servants already working for her in the house, and she's been through all of them, but none of them pleased her as a caregiver." Mama smiled at her. "Truly, it was a blessing I learned about it from Lois down the way. She came by special to tell me—being she's too old and ill for that kind of work."

"A caregiver." Elsie smiled, imagining the position. She'd have to feed and care for a sweet and frail old lady; to tuck her into bed and bring her tea, maybe even read to her. "That sounds perfect, Mama."

"I know." Mama rested a hand on her daughter's cheek, her eyes filling with love. "You do so love to care for people. You would be good at this."

"What do I have to do?" Elsie asked. "Must I go there to see if the job is mine?"

"Certainly, you must – they will have to interview you, and you might not get the job," Mama cautioned. "But I have a feeling you will. First, though, you'll need to be a little more presentable."

"What do you mean?"

"I mean that tomorrow, my dear, we'll be taking the savings that I keep hidden under my mat and going shopping." Mama grinned, genuine joy in her eyes. "And we're going to buy you a nice new dress so that you look like the little lady I know you are."

"A new dress?" Elsie's heart leaped. "Are you sure?"

"Yes, I'm quite sure." Mama leaned forward and kissed Elsie tenderly on her forehead. "You deserve it, my lovely child. We'll go and pick out something that you like, just especially for your big interview."

Elsie wrapped her arms around her mother. "Thank you, Mama," she whispered.

Her eyes filled with tears as she felt the rough, patched fabric of her mother's dress chafe against her. She wished that she could bring her mama all the food and clothing that she could ever need. As Mama returned her embrace, and Elsie buried her face deeply into her mother's neck, she vowed to herself that she was going to get that job. She was going to make her mother's life better.

CHAPTER 2

"Careful, Mama," said Elsie, clinging tightly to her mother's arm. "It's windy today."

Mama gave a little laugh as they stepped out of the tenement. "It's not going to blow me over, child," she said.

Elsie wasn't so sure. Mama looked so light and fragile in the morning sun; her skin was so pale that Elsie could see a pattern of blue veins in her cheeks. Her hand was bony where she clutched Elsie's arm, and already she was breathing a little quickly from the walk down the hall. But her eyes were bright, and she looked over at Elsie with a smile. They were almost the same height, she realized with a jolt.

"All right," Elsie said, returning the smile. "If you say so – let's go!"

They ventured out onto the street, Mama still holding tightly to Elsie's arm. She was grateful that they were walking through the ugly streets early in the morning. Somehow, the golden light just after dawn painted the dark slum in kinder colors; the expressions of the people walking in the street looked a little gentler, and the wind seemed to have cleaned the air of the stench that always hung above the grubby streets.

Elsie wanted to walk quickly to get out of the slums and into the nicer market area of the city. She knew that the dirty slum always made Mama feel sad and hopeless. But Mama's legs couldn't keep up with Elsie's, and so she had to walk slowly, trying not to look at the sad and filthy details that surrounded them.

After a few minutes' walking, Mama spoke. "I wish something could be done about all this rubbish in the street," she said. "Look at that. It must be weeks old."

She pointed at the rotting skeleton of a cat lying in the street, its flesh sunken and shriveled between the tiny bones, some of them stripped of skin and gleaming yellow-white.

"Don't look at it, Mama." She searched the street, seeking a single beautiful thing in the morning light, and found it right on the corner. Pausing, Elsie bent down to touch the petals of a single dandelion blooming in a crack between the cobblestones. It was as soft as a breath on her fingertips. "Look at this," she said. "Isn't it lovely?"

A DAUGHTER'S DESPERATION

Mama smiled, looking down at Elsie. She put an arm around her daughter and pulled her close, planting a soft kiss on her forehead. "Just like you," she said. "A pretty and bright thing, blooming in a horrible place." Her eyes filled with regret. "I wish I could give you a better life, Elsie. You deserve more than this."

"I've got you, Mama." Elsie took her mother's hand and gripped it warmly. "Besides, I'm going to get us both a better life, you'll see." She gave an excited little giggle. "Once I've gotten my beautiful new dress."

Mama laughed. "I wish I could buy satin and lace for you, my love."

"Wool will do just fine." Elsie smiled. "It'll be warmer than silly old satin."

Mama squeezed Elsie's hand. "Thank you."

"What for?"

"For being such a happy little thing." Mama smiled. "Agnes Whiston won't have a choice but to hire you. You're quite irresistible."

"Especially in my new dress!" grinned Elsie.

Mama laughed. "You'd think you were getting a taffeta ball gown, the way you're carrying on."

"I'm just excited, that's all," said Elsie. "Look – we're at the shop already." She saw her mother's fast breathing and how

17

pale her face was, and worry filled her. But she knew she had to be cheerful. "The walk wasn't so bad, was it then?"

"No, it wasn't so bad," panted Mama. "Not at all."

Elsie still felt a little worried, but she kept her arm steady for Mama to hold onto and walked up to the door of the shop. Its sign called it a secondhand clothing shop, but Elsie knew that most of the clothes inside had had at least three or four owners. Still, it had been a long time since she'd worn anything except the ragged dress she had on, and she had grown so much since then that the skirt was a few inches too short and the shoulders pinched.

Pushing the door open, Elsie heard a bell jingle above her head. It was quiet inside, but warmer out of the wind, and poorly lit; she felt a moment of worry, and then a male figure emerged from behind the counter and a candle was lit. Its flickering flame illuminated a kind little old face, as brown and wrinkled as a goblin's, but with gentle eyes.

"Dear Mrs. Griggs." The old man hurried out from behind the counter to wring Mama's hand happily. "I haven't seen you in so long."

"Mr. Brown." Mama smiled. "You haven't aged a bit."

Mr. Brown chuckled. "It's hard to age more once you're past seventy," he said. "It's been a while since you were in here for the young master's shoes. How is he?"

Mama's face fell a little. "Philip couldn't come today," she said, carefully skirting the question. "Instead, we're here for a dress for Elsie." She smiled, putting an arm around Elsie's shoulders.

"A dress." Mr. Brown clapped his hands in joy. Elsie noticed that he only had three fingers on his right hand. "Well, you've come to the right place, my dear. I may be only a secondhand shopkeeper now, but I was a master tailor in my day, you know." He waggled the three fingers left on his hand. "Until I lost my thumb and forefinger in an accident, that is."

"Don't you miss tailoring?" asked Elsie as Mr. Brown took her hand and led her into the circle of light cast by the candle.

He looked at her for a moment, his head on one side, summarizing her with a friendly look. "Oh, I do, a little," he said. "But now I get to make girls like you feel like – princesses." He raised her hand in his own and gave her a little spin. Elsie giggled, feeling her dirty dress swish around her legs. "Now, I don't have a great variety, my dear Elsie," said Mr. Brown. "But first answer me this – what color do you like?"

"Mr. Brown." Mama stepped forward and laid a hand on his arm. "I'm afraid we'll just have to take the cheapest that we can fit to her."

"Please, Mrs. Griggs." Mr. Brown turned to Elsie and winked at her. "Did you know, my dear, that your mother used to be a housekeeper?"

"I do," said Elsie. "But then she got sick."

"Yes, she did, and it was a tragedy," said Mr. Brown, "when she could no longer work. But in her young days, having just been married to your papa, she was the housekeeper at a beautiful manor where I once worked. And after my accident, she was the only soul in the world who was still good to me. It was a very, very sad day for me when she became too frail and sickly to work there anymore." He turned back to Mama. "So for you, Mrs. Griggs, whatever you have in your hand, you can pay for any dress that I have in this shop."

"You are too kind," Mama began, tears filling her eyes.

"Hush, hush! None of that," said Mr. Brown. "Now, Elsie. I asked you a question." His eyes sparkled. "What color?"

"Do you have anything in green?" asked Elsie.

"For the daughter of Mrs. Griggs, I wish I had lace in lime green and silk in an emerald hue," said Mr. Brown with an eloquent bow. "But I daresay I might have a little something for you." He bounced toward the racks at the back of the shop. After a few seconds, he came back, carrying several dresses draped over his arm.

For the next hour, Elsie tried on one dress after the other, and the little shop was filled with laughter. Some of the dresses had many patches, others were itchy and scratched; still others held the lingering smell of their old owners, clinging to the fabric like ghosts of the past. None of them really fit, but with every dress that she slipped over her head, Elsie felt a thrill of excitement. And every time she stepped out of the changing room and saw the pride in her mother's eyes, then heard the happy exclamations of Mr. Brown as he moved around her and gazed at her as if she was the most beautiful thing he'd ever seen, Elsie felt more and more like a princess.

At last, she settled on a cotton dress that had been bottle green once. Its color had faded now, but there were miraculously no patches on it, and it sat softly on her skin like the embrace of an old friend.

"You look wonderful," said Mama, smiling at Elsie as she twirled this way and that, feeling the warmth and weight of the material moving around her hips.

"You look like a duchess," said Mr. Brown, gallantly kissing Elsie's hand, "or like an opera singer."

Elsie laughed. "I think I'm a little too skinny for that, Mr. Brown."

"Elsie Griggs." Mr. Brown held her hand warmly and gave her a steady, serious look out of sparkling eyes. "Never let anybody tell you that you're a little too anything to be anyone."

Elsie was still trying to decipher this sentence as Mama put her handful of coins on the counter. "We'll leave you her old dress, too," she said. "This is hardly enough for what you've just given her."

"Mrs. Griggs, don't be ridiculous," said Mr. Brown, sweeping the coins quickly into his pocket.

Elsie saw Mama's eyes travel over Mr. Brown's threadbare jacket and the place on his left shoe where the sole was coming loose, showing a glimpse of white flesh. "Mr. Brown," she began.

"Hush, my dear." Mr. Brown touched her arm. "Peace now. It's the least I can do for you."

Mama relented. "Thank you," she said, putting an arm around Elsie's waist. "You picked a perfect dress for my beautiful daughter." She grinned at Elsie. "I should think you're rather too grand to live with the likes of me, Miss Griggs."

Elsie laughed. "Mama, please."

"Perhaps I should call you ma'am instead." Mama pinched her cheek lovingly. "You look like you should be living in a fancy house while I wait on you hand and foot."

Elsie wrapped her arms around her mother and kissed her cheek. "Don't be ridiculous, Mama. I would never let that happen, not even if I was the Queen."

Linking arms, Elsie and her mother headed out of the shop and back toward their tenement. Elsie's new dress swished merrily as she walked, and she felt as though everything was just a little lighter, the streets a little cleaner, the sunshine a little brighter, even the air a little clearer. Because tomorrow, she was going to go up to Whiston Manor, and she was going to get that job and make Mama's life better. She knew it.

She just knew it.

CHAPTER 3

The door to the tenement was open a crack. The thin wind whistled through the gap between the door and its crumbling frame, hissing and whispering ominously.

"Mama." Scared, Elsie grabbed her mother's arm. "We locked the door behind us, didn't we?"

"We did." Mama touched the key, which hung on a string around her neck. She squared her shoulders, but Elsie could see that her face was pale. "Don't worry, Elsie. I don't think anyone would break in – what do we have to steal?"

There was a low thump from inside the tenement, and a floorboard creaked. Elsie pulled Mama back. "There's somebody in there, Mama. Come away. It's not safe."

Mama took a hesitant step back, her eyes widening. "Who's there?" she called out, her voice quivering.

The door banged open. Both Elsie and Mama jumped, and an angry-eyed, tousle-haired young man stood in the doorway, his mouth twisted into an angry scowl. "It's just me," he spat. "Don't be daft."

Elsie's shoulders sagged with relief.

"Philip!" cried Mama, a smile spreading across her features. "You frightened me, dear." She rushed over to him, but Philip turned away, pushing her hands aside. "Don't," he growled.

Elsie saw Mama's heartbreak in her eyes, but she didn't say anything. "Where have you been, love?" Mama asked, following Philip inside. Elsie came in and shut the door behind them.

"Out," snapped Philip. "And you? Where were you? I've hardly ever seen you leave the tenement." He raked Mama with a rough glance, but Elsie saw concern in his eyes behind his anger. "Are you all right?"

"Yes, my dear. I'm fine," said Mama, smiling. "We had to go and get—"

As quickly as the moment of concern had come, it was gone again. Philip gave a disinterested grunt. "Good." He flopped down onto one of the sleeping mats and gestured vaguely in the direction of the table. "I brought food."

Trying not to look desperate, Elsie hurried over to the table and grabbed a newspaper-wrapped parcel from its surface. It was tied with dirty string, and as she struggled to untie it, she realized how hungry she was. The string sprang loose, and a few potatoes tumbled onto the table, accompanied by two carrots and a single, lonely beet.

"Philip." Mama sounded delighted. "This is wonderful, dear. I'll make us some soup."

"Please, not soup *again*," Philip moaned. "It's always soup around here, if it isn't gruel."

"It's what we've got, Philip," said Elsie, a little annoyed. "What else do you expect us to make with this?"

"Hush now, Elsie." Mama grabbed a matchbox from the mantelpiece and knelt by the fire. "We'll boil them up whole and eat them that way. I think we've still got a little salt somewhere – it'll be grand. Wash those potatoes for us, dear."

Swishing the potatoes around in water so cold it stung her fingertips, Elsie glanced over at Philip. Slumped on the sleeping mat, he stared at nothing. He had a week's worth of stubble on his chin, and the moody light in his eyes was becoming all too familiar. Elsie found herself wondering why he'd even come back. She stopped herself. He was her brother, and she loved him, and he had once been a playful, happy companion for her – back in long-forgotten days when Papa was still alive, and Mama had worked as a housekeeper.

"You were asking where we'd been all morning," Elsie said hopefully.

Philip looked up, disinterested. "So?"

"Well." Elsie took a deep breath and stepped in front of him, grasping at her skirt to spread it out. She turned from side to side, swishing the warm green fabric so that it rustled. "What do you think?"

Philip stared at her. "Of what?"

Elsie felt the crack in her heart like it was something physical. Her hands fell to her sides, and she looked down at the dress. Suddenly it looked like a cheap thing, well-worn, ordinary, where only moments ago it had felt like a princess's finest gown.

"Philip." Mama's tone was reproachful.

Philip stared at her blankly. "What?" he demanded. "What have I done wrong now?"

Mama gave him an intent look. "Her dress," she muttered.

Philip stared back at Elsie, his brow furrowed. "Oh," he said. "Right."

Trying to hold back tears, Elsie hurried back to the table. She plunged the carrots into the water, watching it turn brown where it rinsed the soil from them. "Elsie..." Philip began.

"It's nothing," said Elsie quickly, her hands trembling as she broke the roots off the beet and swished it in the water. "It's – it's an old thing." She smoothed the front of the dress quickly with one hand. "I'm not surprised you didn't notice."

"Elsie." Philip got up, one rough hand awkwardly brushing Elsie's arm. "It's nice. I like it."

His voice was flat. When Elsie looked up into his eyes, they were pleading, but she could see that he didn't have the energy – or the motivation – to say more. She tried to smile for him.

"Thank you. Mama bought it for me this morning." She grinned at the memory, and a little magic seemed to seep back into the dress's fibers, making it sparkle just a little where it rested on her skin. "The man at the shop was so nice. He said he was an old friend of Mama's."

"Mr. Brown, dear," Mama chipped in, dropping the potatoes into the pot on the fireplace. "I'm sure you'll remember him, Philip. He used to stop by sometimes for dinner before…" Mama paused, taking a sharp breath. "Before your father passed on."

Philip's expression darkened. He said nothing for a few moments.

"Do you remember?" Mama prompted.

Philip raised one shoulder in a non-committal half-shrug. "Maybe," he grunted.

In silence, Elsie helped her mother to boil the vegetables. It was only once she'd brought out their tin plates and Mama was scooping out the pale, gleaming vegetables that Elsie managed to find the courage to speak again. "How – how was your day, Philip?"

"Fine," grunted Philip, taking his plate and flopping into one of the rickety chairs by the table.

Mama glanced over at Elsie, and she saw pity in her mother's eyes. Turning to Philip, Mama spoke. "Don't you want to know why we bought your sister such a lovely new dress?"

Philip stuffed a forkful of potato into his mouth, shrugging. "Hmm?" he grunted.

"There's a very promising position available at Whiston Manor," said Mama, growing an inch with pride. "Old Agnes Whiston needs a personal maid and caregiver, and Elsie is just the perfect person for the job."

Philip frowned. "Elsie's getting a job?"

"Yes, I am," said Elsie, a bubble of excitement rising inside her again. "I'm going to get a real job, and Mama says I'll be good at it. And I'll bring home some money for Mama." She beamed.

Philip wasn't looking at her. "You used to say that no child should have to work before they'd had an education," he said accusingly.

Mama reached over for his hand. "Philip, things have changed."

He snatched his hand away. "Things have changed? That's an understatement." He lurched to his feet, grabbing the remnants of his potato in one hand. Tucking it into his breast pocket, he pushed his chair away and stormed toward the door.

"Philip!" Mama jolted to her feet, grabbing his arm. "I'm sorry. Yes, I never wanted either of you to have to work. I wanted you to improve yourself and become – better than I am. Better than I was." Her eyes were wide, filling slowly with tears. "Please, don't be cross. I just want the best for you." She glanced back at Elsie. "For both of you."

Philip sagged. It seemed as though he shrank two inches as he stood there. He laid a hand on Mama's shoulder, sorrow and anger twisting his features. "I'm not cross, Mama."

"What is it, then?" Mama pleaded.

Philip's eyes wandered through the tenement, and Elsie saw them resting on the two coals in the hearth, the missing floorboard, the chair with only three legs. The dirt and the cold and the dark.

"I don't know," he said, pushing Mama away. He reached for the door. "I just don't know."

It slammed behind him, and Mama sighed. Getting up from the table, Elsie went over to her and put her arms around her waist. "Don't be sad, Mama," she whispered, feeling tears gather thickly in her own throat. "It'll be all right. Philip's only sad about everything that happened."

"I know, my love." Mama kissed the top of Elsie's head, stroking her thick hair. "Don't listen to him. I'm very proud of you, all right?"

"I know." Elsie smiled.

They stood together, still locked in their embrace, for a few long moments. Then Elsie whispered, "Mama?"

"Yes, dear?"

"Everything is going to be fine." Elsie hugged her mother tightly. "I'm going to make our lives good again. I'm going to do everything I can to make everything better."

Mama kissed her again. "You already do, my dear," she said.

CHAPTER 4

It was only about an hour's walk to Whiston Manor, but to Elsie, it felt like she was walking into an entirely foreign country. Leaving the marketplace far behind, Elsie found herself in a neighborhood she'd never even seen before. It reminded her a little of the time when her mother had been a housekeeper, although she didn't remember the buildings being quite so grand as the ones between which she was walking right now. She was thankful Mama had explained the directions so carefully, or she would surely get lost.

The street was perfectly clean – cleaner than the floor of her tenement. There were towering walls and fences around all of the houses, and they loomed on either side of her, massive and grand. They had turrets and chimneys and tall glass windows that reflected the sunlight, dazzling Elsie as she gazed up at them, trying not to look too awestruck. There were elegant lamp-posts everywhere, and trees growing beside the houses with birds singing in them. She had never seen so many archways, so many gabled windows, or so many perfect buildings with not a single brick out of place.

Whiston Manor was at the very end of the street. Elsie's legs were starting to ache with effort as she approached it, her hands clammy with nerves. There was a great brick archway built over a wrought-iron gate with imposing gargoyles snarling down at her from the very top; the name of the manor was displayed proudly across the arch in huge bronze letters, and through the gates Elsie could see a paved driveway swooping off down the hill between manicured green lawns lined with dark pine trees. At the end of the drive, at the very bottom of the hill, stood the manor. Even from here, Elsie could see that it was the biggest and grandest of all the houses on the street. The gates were slightly open, and it took her a long moment standing outside to muster the courage to walk through.

She avoided the drive and took a little footpath instead; it was a winding route, taking her around the lawns and through a huge vegetable garden with stables around the back of it, but she remembered that Mama had told her not to ever walk down the drive. She had to go to the servants' entrance at the back of the house. The smell of compost and manure touched her senses as she picked her way toward the narrow little door right at the very back of the grand house. There were paddocks here, and a deep orchard. Elsie could see the white shapes of some geese beneath the trees, while two horses stood up to their knees in grass, swishing their tails at the flies.

Reaching the servants' entrance, Elsie paused on the threshold to gaze back at the garden and the lawns and the orchard and the paddocks, and her heart missed a beat. It was all so beautiful here. Behind the orchard, she caught a glimpse of a little cottage, overrun with creepers that bloomed in deep purple profusion. She smiled, feeling the nervousness leach out of her heart. This place was peaceful and beautiful – she just knew that she was going to get the job, and she was going to love it here.

Turning back to the doorway, she lifted a hand and knocked. Almost at once, the door was yanked open, and Elsie stared up at what looked like a skeleton wearing a dress and apron. The woman was so thin and gaunt that her eyes had sunken deep into her skull, so deep that Elsie couldn't make out their color in the shadows of her sockets, only a malevolent glimmer suggesting that there were eyes in there at all. Her hair was flint gray and pulled back into a bun so tight that it seemed to be pulling on her upper lip, which was half lifted in a disdainful sneer, revealing yellowed teeth. Despite herself, Elsie had to take a step back, her heart pounding.

"And what do you want?" demanded the apparition.

Elsie stammered wordlessly.

"Spit it out, then," snapped the skull-woman. "I haven't got all day to hang around and watch you blather. Look at the size of this house." She gesticulated angrily. "It's not easy being the housekeeper around here."

Housekeeper. Like Mama. This was the woman that Elsie was supposed to see. She took a deep breath, calming a little. "Um, ma'am, my name is—"

"I don't care what your name is," said the housekeeper impatiently. "I asked what you wanted. Don't waste my time."

"Ma'am, I heard that there was a position available here." Elsie scraped together her courage. "As a personal maid and caregiver."

The housekeeper studied her. "Yes?"

"I was wondering if the position was still open."

The woman snorted. "Of course, it's still open. No girl in her right mind would ever want to take it – the last one ran out crying."

Crying? Elsie pushed the fear out of her mind and tried a winning smile. "Well, ma'am, I would like to apply."

"You would?" The housekeeper frowned. "What's your name then?"

"Elsie. Elsie Griggs."

"And how old are you?"

Elsie paused. Her mother had told her to say that she was

fourteen, but she didn't really want to lie to her prospective new employer. To her relief, the housekeeper shrugged. "Not that it matters. Come into the kitchen and wait here while I go and see if Miss Agnes is at all disposed to see the likes of you." She glared at Elsie as she shut the door behind her. "And if you steal anything, I'll cut off your fingers myself."

Elsie clasped her hands behind her back as she waited. The kitchen was enormous and empty; she could see a ham hanging somewhere in the shadows of the rafters, and a few vegetables were lying on the table, but otherwise there was almost nothing inside. She wondered if Agnes lived in this huge old house all by herself – well, herself and her scary-looking housekeeper. Although the housekeeper seemed to be more scared of Agnes than anything else.

Elsie trembled a little. Why had the last girl run off crying? What was this Agnes really like? She had been picturing a portly little old lady with round spectacles and a bubbling laugh, and she grabbed onto that image, clinging to it against the fear.

Footsteps in the hallway made her jump, and the housekeeper stomped into the kitchen. "Still here, are you?" she said. "Well, the old bat says she'll see you now."

Elsie didn't know what to say, so she said nothing. The housekeeper glared at her for a few moments longer, then snorted, turned on her heel, and stamped off down the hallway. Elsie broke into a near jog to keep up, sticking close behind the housekeeper as they made their way along what felt like more miles of hallway than there were streets in London. The housekeeper walked so fast that Elsie barely had time to take in any of it; she saw only a blur of deep carpets, portraits on the walls glaring down at her with disapproving eyes, even a suit of armor propped up in one corner, its surface gleaming, a halberd clutched in the gauntlet. Elsie tried not to look at its notched blade. It looked as though it had been used, really used, in some battle many years ago.

It seemed to take an age to get anywhere, but at last, the housekeeper stopped abruptly by a pair of elegant wooden doors. She knocked once, sharply. When there was no response, the housekeeper gently pushed the door open and peered inside.

"Oh, good," she said. "She's asleep. In you go."

Elsie found herself being more or less shoved into the room. She caught a glimpse of an old, gray-haired figure lying in a deep armchair, her eyes closed. Elsie turned around quickly. "If she's asleep, what should I—"

But the housekeeper had already gone. The door shut with a gentle thump, and Elsie was all on her own in this enormous room with the sleeping woman.

Turning slowly, Elsie stared around the room. It must have been bigger than the Griggs family's entire tenement, even including the dirty little bathroom at the end of their narrow hallway. The ceiling seemed so high, towering above Elsie's head; the walls were luxuriously draped and covered with patterned wallpaper, and there were numerous lamps on the pillared walls, yet they didn't seem capable of dispelling the shadows that lurked in all the corners despite the fact that it was midday.

The fireplace at the end of the room could have contained Elsie's entire sleeping mat and then some. It roared cheerfully, making Elsie sweat. A patterned hearthrug lay in front of it, and occupying the rug was a preposterously fat ginger cat. When Elsie stared at it, it raised its head and gave her a slow look out of two bright green eyes. Blinking once, it seemed to dismiss her and lowered its head back onto its paws to return to its stately repose.

The same description could not be applied to the old woman. She was slumped in an armchair, one of many luxuriously embroidered pieces of furniture arranged throughout the parlor. The chair looked old and worn, and so did its occupant; it seemed as though she might have been born in that chair and lived in it and fused to it somehow over the decades. Her hair was white, and even though she was asleep, it was still neatly tied back and put up, not a single hair out of place. The lines of her face could have been severe or ready to smile – Elsie couldn't tell; they were slack with sleep, but there was something ominous about the downward slant to her mouth, which was slightly open as she slept. She did not snore. She looked like a sack of human flesh, loosely containing a few dry bones, carelessly cast aside on the chair and left there for the ages to claim as their own.

In the corner of the room, there was a giant grandfather clock. It loomed where it stood, shadows clinging to its edges, and the wooden designs above its face looked like disapproving brows drawn down over the eyes in an unhappy glare. Uncomfortable with staring at the old woman, Elsie stared at the clock instead. Its slow, mournful ticking was the only sound in the room except for the snapping of the fire.

Elsie stood very still, acutely aware of the fact that her beautiful new dress felt suddenly patched and faded in the face of the richly embroidered fabrics of the room around her. Her feet ached a little from the long walk she'd just taken, but she didn't dare to move. Something about the housekeeper's attitude made her think that waking the old woman, whom she presumed to be Mrs. Whiston, would be disastrous. She found herself irresistibly staring at the old woman's face again.

The lines in her skin were deep with age, and there was a bluish tinge on her lips and cheeks. Compassion stirred in Elsie's heart. Mrs. Whiston looked old – old and sick, and she probably needed a personal maid for that very reason. She wasn't that scary, was she? Elsie thought of how quickly the old lady must have fallen asleep, considering that the housekeeper had spoken to her only a few minutes ago.

Smiling to herself, Elsie decided that the spooky old house wasn't going to change the way that she thought about Mrs.

Whiston. She was just a lonely old lady with failing health who needed a friend and a helping hand. She and Elsie were going to get along just—

Suddenly, Mrs. Whiston's eyes snapped open. The old lady shot suddenly as straight and upright as the barrel of a gun on a soldier's arm. Her eyes were as green as the frozen sea, and they bored straight into Elsie, seeming to drill right through her and into her heart, striking it with shards of ice. Elsie jumped despite herself. Trying to get a grip, she stood still, her hands clasped behind her, and waited for Mrs. Whiston to speak first.

But she didn't. Instead, she continued to stare at Elsie, motionless as the suit of armor they'd passed in the hallway. It took Elsie a long moment to find her tongue.

"H-hello," she stammered. "I-I'm Elsie. I'm here to, um, to interview." She swallowed. "For the position, I mean. Of being your personal maid...?" Her voice trailed off, her courage scuttling off into the shadows like a frightened mouse.

Mrs. Whiston's eyes narrowed. "Did you wake me, child?"

"N-no, ma'am."

"You must have woken me." Mrs. Whiston snorted like an irritated horse. "You're the only living thing in this room, aren't you?"

Elsie couldn't help giving the cat a sidelong glance. It returned the look, turning an ear in her direction.

"Don't you even dare to look over at Albert," snapped Mrs. Whiston. "Don't even think about it. He would never dare to awaken me. I've had him seventeen years, and he's never woken me, not once." Her glare intensified. "It must have been you. It could only have been you, you little ragamuffin."

Elsie swallowed. "I'm so sorry, ma'am," she whispered. "I-I was trying to stand as quietly as I could."

"Stand quietly? Well, if you call a herd of stampeding elephants 'quiet', then I suppose you succeeded." Mrs. Whiston folded her arms, her movements vigorous, with no trace of the sickliness that Elsie had thought she'd seen earlier. "Although I suppose I wouldn't be standing quietly either if I was you – wearing that lousy thing. It must be crawling with all manner of bugs."

Elsie laid her hands on her dress, defensively smoothing down the front of the skirt. "It's new, ma'am," she said quickly.

"New? About as new as that grandfather clock standing in the corner," said Mrs. Whiston. "About as new as the carpet you're standing on, which my great-great-grandfather brought out of Persia for my great-great-grandmother. It's too valuable for you to even look at, you silly girl."

Elsie somehow resisted the urge to look down. She kept her eyes fixed on Mrs. Whiston, aware that she was trembling where she stood. The old lady glared at her for a little longer before asking, "And what are you doing here?"

"I came to interview for the position, ma'am," said Elsie in a small voice.

"Position? What position?"

"As your personal maid and caregiver, ma'am."

"I know very well which position, you stupid girl," said Mrs. Whiston. "What are you just standing there for? Tell me what you can do."

The question caught Elsie off guard. She interlaced her fingers to stop her hands from shaking. "Well, ma'am, I can cook and do laundry."

"I want a maid," snapped Mrs. Whiston. "Not a cook or a washerwoman. Get out."

"Wait!" Elsie's heart hammered. She stepped forward, trying not to sound as desperate as she was. "That's not all."

Mrs. Whiston glared at her but didn't stop her from speaking. Trying to pull together her scattered thoughts was like catching a pile of leaves caught by the wind. Elsie stuttered. "I, ah, I could, I-I mean..." She closed her eyes and took a deep breath. "I'm very good at looking after people," she said at last. "I can make sure that you're always warm enough in winter and cool enough in summer. I can read, and I'll soon get to know when you need tea or something to eat and bring it to you."

Mrs. Whiston's frown deepened. "I catch a chill very quickly, you know," she said angrily. "And my constitution is very delicate. My great-great-great-aunt is descended from the Duke of Essex, you know."

Elsie didn't know what to say. "I-I'm sure I'll learn what suits you, ma'am."

"I must also be bathed once a week," Mrs. Whiston went on. "And my bed needs to be made exactly right, or I will catch a chill. Only the best eiderdown may be used," she added severely. "And no Kashmir. Under no circumstances may my skin come into contact with Kashmir."

"Yes, of course, ma'am," said Elsie, who had never heard of Kashmir before.

"And you had better not have cold hands," Mrs. Whiston said. "I cannot abide being touched by cold hands. And no warm hands, either. The girl I had previously had such warm hands – goodness! I nearly died. It was terrible, I tell you." She gathered her shawl a little more tightly around her throat. "I also won't have thieves in my house," she said. "Not a thing may go missing. This house is full of the most priceless heirlooms – things that you could hardly even comprehend the value of."

"Of course not, ma'am."

"Of course not?" Mrs. Whiston bridled. She drew herself up as angrily as a cobra. "*Of course not?* Of course *nothing*, you little snipe. You couldn't know anything about any of these priceless treasures in this house. How dare you even suggest such a thing? My family has the *most* discerning taste — nothing like *yours*."

Elsie felt a lump gathering in her throat. This wasn't going the way she had planned. "I-I'm sorry," she stammered. "I didn't mean—"

Mrs. Whiston dismissed her with a little wave of her hand. "Stop blathering," she ordered. "Go and fetch me some tea."

"Excuse me?" said Elsie.

"*Tea*, you little idiot," said Mrs. Whiston. "Tea!"

Elsie froze. What was this supposed to mean? Was it a test of some type?

"Go!" snapped Mrs. Whiston.

The word made Elsie jump into action. She scurried off, closing the door of the parlor behind her, and hurried toward the kitchen. For a few panicky moments, she thought she had gotten lost, but she finally found her way back down into the kitchen. A middle-aged woman with greasy hair was now listlessly prodding at a large pot on the stove; the housekeeper sat by the fire with her feet up on a stool. They both looked up as Elsie came in.

"Well?" demanded the housekeeper. "What are you waiting for? You know where the door is. Off you go."

"I, um, actually it seems..." Elsie stammered.

"Push off." The housekeeper turned back to the fire. "There's nothing we can do for you now, girl."

"Tea," Elsie managed.

The cook and housekeeper stared at her.

"Mrs. Whiston would like some tea," said Elsie, more clearly. "If you would give me some to take to her, please."

The cook and housekeeper exchanged a surprised glance. The housekeeper gave a little snort and got to her feet. "Well, what are you waiting for, Florence?" she demanded of the cook. "You heard what the girl said – the mistress wants her tea." With that, she flounced out of the room.

Florence turned to Elsie and gave her a warm smile as she poured some tea into a cup and set it on a tray. "You must be hired then, dear," she said.

"I-I don't know, to be honest," said Elsie, put at ease somewhat by the cook's gentle expression. "She was shouting at me and then she just said she wanted tea."

"That's the mistress for you, love," said the cook, pressing the tray into Elsie's hands. "Congratulations."

As Elsie made her way back toward the parlor, the teacup rattled in the saucer as her hands trembled. But the further she walked, the more her hands steadied, and a smile began to spread over her features.

"I have a position," she whispered to herself, feeling joy

bubble up inside of her. "I have a *position*. I knew it would happen. And it did!"

She couldn't wait to get home and tell her mother. But first – Agnes Whiston wanted her tea. So Elsie trained her eyes on the cup and made her way as carefully as she could to the parlor, determined to do her job right. She'd been given this chance, and she was going to take it.

CHAPTER 5

"Mama! Mama!" Elsie burst into the tenement, breathless. She had run most of the way back from Whiston Manor. "You won't believe it."

Mama flew up from the sleeping mat where she had been sitting. Her face blanched as she looked at Elsie, and she swayed. For a moment, Elsie thought she would fall. She rushed across the room, grabbing Mama's arm.

"Mama!" she cried, worried. "Whatever is the matter?"

Mama leaned her head on Elsie's shoulder for a moment, then took a deep breath and straightened. "Nothing, my dear." Her face was still pale as she wrung out a smile. "Just a little dizzy spell, that's all."

Elsie stared at her mother for a long moment. She was so

pale, and Elsie noticed that her hands and face were bonier than ever; it was as if the flesh was simply shrinking away, dissolving from her mother's bones. But now she could do something about it. She was going to make Mama's life better.

"Are you sure you're all right?" she asked.

"Yes, yes, of course." Mama touched Elsie's cheek. "Now what has got you into such a flap, my dear? You sounded like a herd of elephants coming down the hall."

"You're sure," Elsie said reluctantly.

"Yes, my dear!" Mama laughed. "Enough now. Tell me what's gotten you so excited."

Elsie's glad news overwhelmed her for a second. She took a deep breath, and the words spilled out all at once. "I got the position, Mama," she said. "I got the job at Whiston Manor!"

"Oh, Elsie." Mama reached out and pulled Elsie into her arms. "Congratulations, love. I'm so proud of you."

"Thanks, Mama." Elsie pulled back, still grinning. "Things are going to be so much better now. We're going to have at least one meal every single day and we're not going to worry about the rent at all anymore. And – and when you're sick, maybe we could even get you to the doctor."

"Slowly, slowly," said Mama, grinning. She placed her hands on Elsie's shoulders, staring down at her with eyes that were filled with love. "You're a personal maid now, Elsie, not a lady of the manor. But yes, for sure, things are going to be easier."

"I'm going to do everything I can to help you," said Elsie softly.

"I know, my dear." Mama planted a tender kiss on Elsie's forehead. "Now, tell me all about Whiston Manor and what it's like there."

They sat down together on the sleeping mat as Elsie told Mama about the imposing house, the beautiful grounds, the stern housekeeper, and how strange Mrs. Whiston was.

"She was mean, Mama," said Elsie. "And I didn't even understand half of what she was saying, but she did seem happy when I brought her some tea. I think. I only left when she'd gone back to sleep and the housekeeper told me that I could go."

"And when are you starting?"

"Tomorrow, the housekeeper said." Elsie beamed. "And I'll get paid every week."

"That's wonderful." Mama's eyes grew misty, her voice a little wistful. She put an arm around Elsie's shoulders. "I'm going to miss you, my dear."

"Miss me?" Alarmed, Elsie pulled back. "What do you mean?"

"Well, you'll have to move into the servants' quarters in the manor."

The idea somehow hadn't occurred to Elsie. Immediately, she felt her eyes filling with tears. "But I want to stay here with you."

"I know you do. I truly know." Mama pulled Elsie closer and laid a hand on her cheek, allowing her to nestle into her mother's shoulder. "But you can't make that long walk early in the morning every day, and besides, Agnes might need you in the night."

Elsie nodded slowly, sniffing back her tears. "What about you?"

"I'll be fine here, my love." Mama ran her fingers through Elsie's hair. "I'm sure Philip will be back soon, and besides, I can take care of myself. I'll just miss you, that's all."

"I don't want to go," whispered Elsie.

"I know. But just think of the wonderful room you're going to have, darling." Mama smiled, kissing Elsie's hair. "You're going to have a whole room all to yourself with a proper bed and a window and maybe even a carpet. In such a lovely big house, there won't be any holes in the walls or the roof. It'll be warm and dry and safe."

"I suppose," said Elsie. "But you won't be there."

"Oh, darling." Mama sighed, hugging Elsie a little closer. "I hope with everything in me that someday you will have a far, far better home than this one. I hope you will be free of this place forever soon – and always live somewhere safer, cleaner. Somewhere that you deserve."

There were a few moments of silence. Elsie huddled a little closer against her mother's warm, bony body. She wanted to memorize everything about her: her smell, the color of her hair, the sound of her voice. She had never spent a single night away from her mother before, and she wanted to carry her with her in her mind, as whole and loving as she was right now.

"I'm scared, Mama," Elsie admitted.

"Me too, child," said Mama. "Just a little bit. But I'll pray for you every morning and every night." She stroked some of Elsie's hair out of her face. "Everything will be all right, my dear. You'll see. Everything will be all right."

CHAPTER 6

"Finally, my food absolutely, positively *has* to be served at exactly the right temperature," said Mrs. Whiston. "I simply cannot tolerate hot or cold food. It has to be perfectly warmed. I have a very delicate constitution, on account of my noble blood. My great-great-great aunt was descended from the Duke of Essex."

"Yes, ma'am," said Elsie, having heard that before.

"Don't interrupt me," snapped Mrs. Whiston. "Be quiet and listen. I'm not finished talking yet. It's terribly rude to interrupt – in fact, you may not speak at all unless you need to answer a question. Only 'yes, ma'am' or 'no, ma'am' will be allowed. Do you understand?"

Confused, Elsie nodded.

"Now, what was I saying?" Mrs. Whiston considered this for a second. "Oh, yes. The temperature of my food. Cook knows the temperature that it needs to be when it is ready, and it cools exactly the right amount in twenty-two seconds. Not a second more or less, girl, so it is imperative that you stand waiting in the kitchen for the cook to prepare each dish and bring it straight to me without any form of delay. Twenty-two seconds *precisely*."

Elsie nodded. Her mind felt tired, and her legs were cramping. She had lost track of how long she'd been standing in the middle of the room, listening to Mrs. Whiston's endless tirade of instructions regarding every aspect of her care.

"Well?" Mrs. Whiston glared at Elsie over her half-moon spectacles. "Don't you have anything to say?"

"Um... yes, ma'am?" Elsie attempted.

Mrs. Whiston fixed her for a few moments longer with a steady glare. "Very well." She sniffed. "Now, Mrs. Corbyn will show you to your room and arrange your wages."

"Thank—" Elsie began.

"Don't interrupt me!" Mrs. Whiston glared at her. "Finally, this bell." She reached for a small silver bell on the table beside her armchair and gave it a little ring. Its high-pitched tone was surprisingly loud, ringing around the room and echoing down the empty hallways. "When you hear this bell at any hour of the day or night, you are to come to my assistance immediately – with not a moment's delay."

"Yes, ma'am," said Elsie.

"I may need you in the night, also," said Mrs. Whiston, "so your room is not far from my own. Always be ready should I need you, and I don't want you stumbling in with mussy hair, either. You are expected to be neat and ready to assist me at all hours." She paused. "I am, however, a good and righteous woman, and I will always treat you fairly, so you will have ample time for rest also."

Elsie pricked her ears. *Maybe I will be able to see Mama often, after all,* she thought.

"Between the hours of twelve o' clock and four o' clock on a Sunday afternoon, I will be at repose," said Mrs. Whiston, inclining her head graciously. "You are free to do and go as you please during that time. But ensure you are ready to bring my tea at four o' clock exactly. I must not deviate from my routine. It must be adhered to at all times – with no exceptions."

Elsie's heart sank. "Four hours?" she whispered. "Once a week?"

Mrs. Whiston's eyes flashed. "This is more than enough time," she spat. "Are you contradicting me, girl? Perhaps you do not want this job after all."

"No! No." Elsie wrung her hands. "Not at all, Mrs. Whiston. I do want to work for you very much." She swallowed, thinking fast. "I just wanted to make sure that I had heard right."

Mrs. Whiston looked at her narrowly. "Fine," she said. "Now, Mrs. Corbyn, take her to her room." She waved a dismissive hand. "Allow her to put away her things, but don't be long. My eleven o' clock tea must be brought in exactly on time."

Mrs. Corbyn, the housekeeper, stepped forward and dropped a little curtsy.

"Yes, ma'am," she said. "Come," she added curtly to Elsie, and swept out of the room, once again walking so fast that Elsie could barely keep up. This time, she led her deeper into the mansion, further from the front door. There were rich tapestries and gorgeous paintings on the walls at first, but the further they went from the parlor, the narrower the passages got. Finally, between a few storerooms, they reached a tiny door hidden away in a dark corner.

"Here," sniffed Mrs. Corbyn, unlocking the door.

"Are – do the rest of the servants stay here, too?" asked Elsie.

"No, it's just you," said Mrs. Corbyn. "Mrs. Whiston needs her *personal* caregiver to be close by." She gave Elsie a glare, then pulled the door open.

Elsie stepped into the room. It was tiny—the width of a hallway. There was a narrow bed pushed up against one corner, leaving just enough room for Elsie to shuffle in beside it. A little wooden table was wedged between the bed and the opposite corner, and there was a chest at the foot of the bed for her things. At the head of the bed, a musty gray curtain hung over a square of light that must have been a window.

"There," said the housekeeper. "Put away your things. But be quick about it. The mistress will want her tea right on time."

"Of course," Elsie began, but already the door had slammed behind the housekeeper as she went outside.

Elsie put her cloth bag down on top of the chest, which looked ridiculously large to accommodate her handful of things. The room was almost pitch dark with the door closed, and she felt her way over to the window. Grabbing the curtain, she pulled it open. A cloud of dust rose from the thin material, and Elsie coughed, rubbing it out of her eyes for a moment. When she could see again, she gave a little gasp of delight.

The window looked out on the orchard. From this high floor, Elsie was at the same level as the treetops; their leafy profusion was dark and rich, and tinged with the warm sunlight. Birds sat in every branch, their little voices filling the air as they sang their hearts out. Shining fruits dangled from the boughs, and right by Elsie's window there was a neat little nest fashioned from twigs and bits of grass. There were two eggs in it, beautifully speckled, and as Elsie watched a robin flutter down from another branch to perch on the edge of the nest. Elsie stayed very still as the little bird cocked its head, studying her from a bright, beady eye. Apparently deciding that Elsie was harmless, it hopped into the nest and settled itself down, puffing up its feathers so that it looked fat and content in its home.

"Hello," Elsie whispered softly, smiling. "I'll be your friend – and I think we'll get along just fine."

She stared out at her view, feeling homesick already. She wondered how Mama was doing back at home and if she was going to be all right for the long week that lay ahead. When Mrs. Whiston had told Elsie her wage, she'd been heartbroken at how low it was, but at least she was getting her board – so that would already be helping Mama.

"It won't do to be sad," she whispered to the robin. "I must be grateful for what I have. And since I have this lovely view," she added, "I think I'm quite lucky, don't you?"

The robin just turned its head to look at her, and Elsie smiled. At least she had one little friend in this huge, cold house – and maybe, if she was lucky, she would make more.

***

THE PARLOR WAS FILLED WITH GUESTS, EACH LOOKING MORE distinguished than the next. Elsie trembled, trying not to look as nervous as she was. It was only her third day in her new job, and she still wasn't used to sleeping in the gigantic old house; it creaked and moaned deep in the night, keeping her wide awake as she listened to the echoes of the empty space all around her, feeling pinned down at the same time in her tiny room.

It was the gentleman with the monocle sitting directly opposite Agnes, warming his feet by the fire, that worried Elsie the most. He was so tall and gaunt that, in the flickering firelight, he could have been a skeleton. Most of the time he was looking at Agnes, but every now and then his cold eyes would rest on her where she stood attentively behind Agnes's armchair, and they made her shudder.

"Your parlor is most tastefully decorated, Mrs. Whiston." The speaker was the feminine half of the young couple sitting side by side on the settee facing the fire. She smiled demurely, folding her hands in her lap. "You have an impeccable sense of style."

"Thank you, my dear." Mrs. Whiston preened. "But I can't take all the credit for it, you know. Some of it was done by my ancestors – this house is many years old already."

"It is a most beautiful house," said the young lady.

Mrs. Whiston beamed, and Elsie inwardly breathed a sigh of relief. The old lady was much more amenable if her taste was being praised.

The conversation turned to business matters. Elsie didn't understand much other than that the older gentleman, the frightening one, had invested money in ships that Mrs. Whiston seemed to own. The young couple were related to him somehow. Their talk bored her, and she tried to stay awake where she stood. The parlor was very warm, and she had been up and down the corridor all night as Mrs. Whiston rang the bell every time she so much as tossed and turned.

"You, girl." Mrs. Whiston snapped her fingers, and Elsie straightened, trying to look as alert as possible. "We need some tea. Go down to the kitchen and tell the cook to make us some, and quickly."

"Yes, ma'am." Elsie hurried off. She was finding her way through the house more easily now, although the sheer size of it was still confusing. At last, she reached the kitchen with only one wrong turn and opened the door.

"Florence," she called.

Florence was standing by the oven, checking on the dinner she was making for herself and the other servants – which Elsie knew by experience she'd be eating cold, late, and probably standing up.

"Yes, dear?" she answered.

"The mistress wants some tea sent up."

"All right, dear. I'll send Polly with it."

Relieved that the housemaid would be bringing the tea, Elsie started to hurry back toward the parlor. She knew that Mrs. Whiston hated being left alone. Surely, though, it would be all right this time, considering she'd sent Elsie out on an errand? A knot of nervousness began to gather in Elsie's gut.

When she heard the shouting as she walked up the corridor, she knew she was in trouble. Mrs. Whiston's angry yells were accompanied by the jangling of the little bell, and Elsie broke into a run. She burst into the parlor to see that Mrs. Whiston's face was blotchy purple, almost apoplectic with total rage. Her guests looked more than a little shell-shocked. Albert the cat was perched on the arm of Mrs. Whiston's chair, and, worst of all, her knitted lap-blanket lay on the floor at her feet.

"Get over here, you stupid girl," Mrs. Whiston yelled. "Put this blanket back up at once!" Her eyes were wild with rage.

Elsie hurried to grab the lap-blanket and lifted it back over Mrs. Whiston's knees.

"No!" The old lady's voice was as sharp as a cracking whip. "Not like that. The other way around, you imbecile." She was still yelling even though Elsie was right by her side.

"S-sorry, ma'am," Elsie stammered, struggling to tuck the blanket over Mrs. Whiston's lap.

"Where were you?" Mrs. Whiston demanded. "I told you that I cannot possibly be allowed to catch a chill. My constitution is very delicate. I will catch my death. And it will be your fault."

"I'm s-sorry," Elsie managed. "I-I went to get the tea you asked for."

Mrs. Whiston's eyes looked like they might pop out of her head with anger. "Are you talking back to me?" she growled.

"N-no. No, ma'am," Elsie whimpered. She had no idea what to say or do to avert her employer's rage – much less what she had done to earn it in the first place.

"Don't try to be smart with me," Mrs. Whiston hissed. She grabbed Elsie's dress in an iron grip, pulling her closer. "I expect you to be attending to me *at all times*. That is, after all, your job."

"S-sorry, ma'am," Elsie said. "It won't happen again."

She knew that her hands were shaking. What had she done wrong? She had tried so hard to follow Mrs. Whiston's orders to the letter. She couldn't help but notice the shocked and sympathetic eyes of the couple on the settee. The old man, however, was nodding.

"See to it that it doesn't," Mrs. Whiston spat. "Now don't you dare leave this room, do you understand?"

Elsie's throat was a hot, heavy lump of tears. She nodded mutely and took up her place behind Mrs. Whiston's chair again, hoping that the shadows of the evening would be enough to hide the tears that were slowly running down both of her cheeks.

CHAPTER 7

As Elsie stepped through the doorway of the ugly, decrepit tenement building, the reek of the place filled her nose. It was a familiar, pungent stench born from the mingled smells of bitter gruel, the filthy lavatory, the mold seeping in the corners and cracks, and the nameless and horrible odor filtering in from the street outside. The smell could not be described in a single term, but to Elsie, it was the only smell of home that she knew.

She felt her shoulders sag in relief as she walked down the hallway, her heart beating with anticipation. The manor house smelt of soap and flowers and firewood, but she would take this stinking tenement over it any day because of what lay beyond the door. She pushed the door open, shouting happily. "Mama! I'm home."

"Elsie!"

Elsie had barely stepped into the room when she found herself caught up in her mother's embrace. The thin arms surrounding her were everything she'd been missing all week. She nestled her face into Mama's shoulder and clung to her, breathing her familiar smell in deep gulps. Elsie felt as though she'd been lost in the desert, and Mama's presence was a cup of cool water, and she breathed it with the same desperate eagerness.

"Oh, Elsie." Mama kissed her cheek and pulled back, holding her daughter at arm's length to gaze at her with shining eyes. "You're looking so well. You've been eating well."

"Three meals every day, Mama," said Elsie. "I missed you so, so much."

"Oh, I missed you too, my darling." Mama hugged her again, sighing in relief and happiness. "I missed you, but I'm so glad to see you looking so well."

"I'm feeling well, Mama," said Elsie truthfully. "My room is nice and warm, and I get more than enough to eat. Florence the cook makes sure of that – she's very nice." She held up the basket that she'd been carrying over her arm. "She sent you some bread and even a bit of ham."

Mama's eyes widened, and Elsie felt a tug of sorrow and worry. In the guttering light from a candle on the little table, the shadows of Mama's skeletal body were etched with brutal harshness on her skin; her hollowed cheeks, her bony hands, even the scooped-out spaces beneath her protruding collarbones.

"Have you been eating, Mama?" she murmured.

"Of course, she has." The angry, defensive voice came from the corner of the room. "Do you think she really needed *you*, a twelve-year-old kid, to look after her?"

Startled, Elsie looked up. Philip was standing in the corner, leaning against the wall with his arms folded. He straightened when he saw Elsie looking at him.

"I'm her child, too," he said angrily. "I've been keeping an eye on her now that you're off at your *job* all the time."

"Philip." Elsie grinned. "I'm so glad you're here, too." She stepped forward as if to embrace him, but something in his eyes stopped her. Lowering her head, she added softly, "I've missed you."

Philip relented somewhat. "We've missed you, too," he said gruffly. "Come on. Let's have something to eat."

They sat down around the table while Mama put out their tin plates and forks. They only had one knife. Elsie watched silently as Mama used it to cut the breads, struggling a little as its blunt edge faltered on the crust. She thought of the chests and chests of heirloom silverware that stood around the manor house, untouched for decades. The china plates displayed in glass cases in the hallways. Part of her felt a pang of confusion. How could that be fair?

"There you are." Mama put a chunk of bread and a little slice of ham on each plate. She smiled, and genuine warmth lit up her tired eyes. "Let's say grace."

They sat down together, and Elsie reached for Philip's hand, but he had already interlaced his fingers and closed his eyes. Awkwardly, Elsie folded her hands.

There were a few moments of silence. "Philip?" Mama prompted.

"You do it." Philip's voice was curt.

Another pause stretched; the air filled with such tension that Elsie thought it might twang. Finally, Mama murmured, "For what we are about to receive, may the Lord be thanked. Amen."

"Amen," Elsie repeated.

Philip said nothing. He grabbed the chunk of bread with a dirty hand and started stuffing it hungrily into his mouth. Elsie noticed that he had a stubbly beard and a new bruise just above his left eye. She wondered where her brother had been, what he had been doing all week, because she could see that his sleeping mat was undisturbed.

"How... how have you been?" she asked hesitantly.

Philip shot her a hot glance. "Fine," he grunted.

"What have you been doing?" asked Elsie, trying to get a conversation going.

Philip shot to his feet. His chair squealed across the floor, and Elsie heard something splinter in one of its rickety legs. "What does it matter?" he demanded.

Elsie cringed. "I-I was just asking," she stammered.

"Philip." Mama's voice was exhausted. "Sit down and eat your food. Nobody is trying to annoy you."

Elsie was silent. Philip stood for a few more seconds, then sighed and flopped back into the chair. His voice was a little gentler when he spoke next. "Tell us about your week, Elsie," he said with an attempt at friendliness.

"Yes, do that." Mama smiled and laid a hand over Elsie's. "How is it in the manor house? Have you made some friends?"

"The house is huge." Elsie grinned. "It's beautiful, and warm, and I have a room all my own – close to Mrs. Whiston's so that I can help her during the night."

"Is Mrs. Whiston nice?" asked Mama.

Elsie paused. She didn't want to tell Mama how frightening and cruel she found her employer. "She's a bit scary," she said slowly, "but she's all right."

"And the housekeeper?"

"Mrs. Corbyn is always very cross," said Elsie. "The other

maids don't like me, either, because I don't sleep in the servants' quarters with them. But Florence is nice. She's quiet, but she makes sure we eat well, and she doesn't let Mrs. Corbyn boss her around too much."

Mama's face fell. "I'm sorry, Elsie," she said. "I thought you might make some friends with the other maids. You hardly ever see anyone your own age."

"It's all—" Elsie began, but Philip interrupted her with an angry snort.

"What is it, Philip?" asked Mama.

"What?" demanded Philip.

"I heard you." Mama's voice had sternness beneath its gentleness. "Is there something you need to tell me?"

Philip put his bread back down on his plate and leaned back in his wobbly chair, fixing Mama with a glare. "You do nothing but complain about my friends," he said. "You're always saying that they're trouble, or that I spend too much time with them. But you want Elsie to have friends."

"Philip, I only say those things because your friends drink too much. I'm worried that—" Mama began.

"See?" Philip gestured at her furiously. "You complain about them all of the time. But not about Elsie." He shook his head.

"Don't drag Elsie into this," said Mama. "You know that it's not about her."

"It's always about her, Mama!" Philip slapped his hand down on the table, making Elsie's plate rattle. "Perfect, sweet little Elsie who can do no wrong. What about me?"

"Philip—"

"No." Philip held up a hand. "I don't want to hear it." He got up and grabbed his coat where it hung over the back of his chair.

"Where are you going?" cried Elsie.

"Away," snapped Philip. He shrugged on his coat.

"When are you coming back?" Mama asked.

"I don't know." With that, Philip slammed the door behind him. Paint flaked down from the walls, and when Elsie looked over at Mama, she saw tears in her eyes. Elsie's appetite was gone. She pushed aside her plate, searching for something to make Mama feel better, and took a little cloth pouch from her dress pocket.

"Mama," she said quietly, setting it down on the table.

Mama stared at it numbly. "Your wages?"

"Yes. It's enough for this week's food and rent. The shops were all closed now, but maybe... maybe I can get away to do your shopping, or..."

"It's all right, love." Mama found a smile for Elsie and pressed it on. "Philip will help me."

"Do you think he will?"

"He will. You'll see. He's just..." Mama sighed. "Let's not talk about it." She put an arm around Elsie's shoulders. "Tell me all about your week – and don't leave anything out."

Elsie wanted to ask why Philip was behaving the way that he was, but she didn't want to hurt Mama's heart even more. "Well," she began, "there's a tree just outside my window, and in its branches there's a little red-breasted robin..."

CHAPTER 8

Elsie had seldom seen anything as strangely appalling as Mrs. Whiston's naked body. The old lady wallowed in her bath, a beached white whale thrashing miserably in the warm water, her acreage of stretched and doughy flesh wobbling and rippling as she shifted her position with a series of breathless little grunts.

Elsie shuddered a little, forcing herself to work the soft flannel over Mrs. Whiston's back. She wondered why her mistress even bothered to bath at all. She never went outside, and the house was always scrupulously clean. Even the bathwater was still clean enough to see through – unlike Elsie's.

Still, Mrs. Whiston insisted on being bathed and gently cleaned with a creamy little lavender-scented cake of soap every single week, and woe betide Elsie if she didn't do it exactly right. She gritted her teeth, working the soap into the flabby folds of the back of Mrs. Whiston's neck, trying to be as gentle as she could.

"Come on, girl!" Mrs. Whiston spluttered, breathless with effort. "You need to *clean* that skin. If I get a rash, I will be most put out. I have very delicate skin, you know."

"Yes, ma'am. Sorry, ma'am." Elsie scrubbed a little harder with the flannel, and Mrs. Whiston let out an indignant squawk that made Elsie jump and drop her soap into the bath.

"No!" the old lady cried. "No, no, no! You'll tear my skin off. Have you no consideration for others, you heartless child?"

"Sorry, ma'am." Elsie dived to rescue the soap, fishing it out of the tepid water as quickly as she could. "Almost done."

"Almost done? Almost done? Do you really think you're almost done? You haven't touched my feet yet. Oh, why are you so cruel and ignorant?"

Elsie tried her best to ignore Mrs. Whiston as she rinsed the soap off her mistress's back and then moved on to the part that she hated the most: those feet. Mrs. Whiston probably couldn't see her own feet past the ponderous curve of her belly, and Elsie envied her that privilege. Her feet were flattened by her weight, swollen at the ankles, and equipped with curling yellow toenails that made Elsie shudder just to look at them.

Elsie knelt at the side of the copper bath and, with much fussing and splashing from Mrs. Whiston, succeeded in getting hold of a foot. Holding her breath when the softened, disgusting toenails rubbed against her skin, Elsie clung on to the foot and scrubbed with a soapy pumice stone for all she was worth. Mrs. Whiston shouted instructions and thrashed around, her soapy feet slipping through Elsie's fingers.

The bathwater slopped onto Elsie's new green dress, then cooled on her skin, but she was concentrating too hard on getting those feet clean to feel the cold. It seemed to take an age before Mrs. Whiston's feet were finally cleaned to her satisfaction, and by then, both she and Elsie were out of breath. Mrs. Whiston sat in the bath with red cheeks, her lips pursed as she sucked in her breaths with noticeable effort.

Elsie shook a lock of sweaty hair out of her face and straightened, feeling her back and knees cramp from huddling on the floor. Silently, she grabbed a huge towel from the nearby rail. The towel had been warmed in front of the fire by one of the chambermaids, and its fluffy warmth was so delicious that Elsie wanted to wrap herself up in it and go to sleep. But Mrs. Whiston was glaring at her impatiently, so instead she just stepped nearer and held the towel open.

With much grunting and splashing, Mrs. Whiston succeeded in struggling to her feet. She clung to the rails around the bath and – for an agonizing moment – to Elsie's hair, finally succeeding in seating herself on the edge of the bath. Elsie wrapped her in the towel, and Mrs. Whiston hugged it around herself, panting.

"Hurry up, girl," she snapped. "Dry my feet."

Elsie rubbed the feet quickly with another towel and stuffed them into an enormous pair of slippers. At last, Mrs. Whiston's bulk was persuaded into a soft robe, and Elsie helped her out of the bathroom, relieved that it was over.

"Where would you like to go, ma'am?" she asked in the doorway of the bathroom, clinging to Mrs. Whiston's arm to keep her upright. "Would you like to have a lie-down first?"

"Take me to the parlor," said Mrs. Whiston curtly. "I can't possibly sleep in this state. You've quite upset me with all of your ineptitude."

Elsie wasn't sure what ineptitude was, but she decided it was best not to ask. "Yes, ma'am."

Walking down the hallway with Mrs. Whiston was always something of an ordeal. The old woman was as unsteady on her feet as she was vast, and Elsie sometimes felt like a tiny ant trying to carry a whole biscuit, propping the woman up and offering encouragement as she made her way toward the parlor.

The door was slightly ajar, and Elsie reached for the knob, keeping one hand on Mrs. Whiston's elbow. Mrs. Whiston let out a cry of anger and dismay, grabbing at Elsie's arm with her huge hands. "Are you completely out of your mind, girl?" she shouted. "You'll drop me on the floor. I could break my neck, at my age."

"Sorry, ma'am. Sorry." Elsie quickly returned both her hands to Mrs. Whiston's arm. "It's all right. I've got you."

"Just get me into my chair," moaned Mrs. Whiston piteously.

Elsie used her elbow to gently nudge the door open, her eyes fixed on Mrs. Whiston's feet. "Almost there, ma'am," she said.

"I'm quite dizzy," groaned Mrs. Whiston, taking a shuffling step forward. Elsie kept her eyes on her mistress's slippers, terrified that they might catch on a wrinkle in the carpet. "You'll be all right, ma'am," she said. "Just keep going. We're nearly there, ma'am."

"Don't patronize me," snapped Mrs. Whiston. "I should think I know where I am in my own house, you little—"

"Hello, Grandmother."

Both Mrs. Whiston and Elsie looked up in surprise. Elsie, having spent the past few minutes staring at Mrs. Whiston's dreadful feet, felt as though she was looking directly into the sun. She blinked, momentarily dazzled, as she gazed at the boy standing in front of the parlor's hearth. He was a lanky figure, not far from Elsie's age, with a glossy wing of black hair that fell across his forehead in a neatly combed wave.

Yet it wasn't his elegant form or even the inexpressible shade of his dark green eyes that captured Elsie's attention. It was his smile. It was the first smile she'd seen since she'd left Mama back in the tenement last Sunday, and it was a wonderful thing—a crooked grin that dimpled one side deeper than the other, making the freckles on his cheeks dance, and lighting up the entire room – perhaps the entire world – with its genuine kindness.

Elsie realized that she and Mrs. Whiston were both just standing there, staring. Then Mrs. Whiston snapped out of it.

"Andrew!" she cried, and for a moment, to Elsie's shock, a smile tugged at the corners of her lips too. Then her habitual scowl returned. "It's about time you set foot in this house once more. I haven't seen you in, oh, so long. It must be months, you know. Months – you children are so unkind to me."

"It's good to see you too, Grandmother," said the boy, laughing easily. He stepped closer, holding out his arms. "I'm sorry to have interrupted your bath time."

"I don't know what you mean by dropping by so unexpectedly," grumbled Mrs. Whiston, but she awkwardly embraced Andrew with something that might even have been genuine warmth.

"I was off school a little earlier than usual, and I thought I would walk over and say hello." Andrew stepped back. "I thought you would like to see me."

Elsie helped Mrs. Whiston into her armchair. Settled once

again on her throne, the old lady gave Andrew a long look before uttering a sigh and extending a magnanimous hand toward the settee.

"I do like to see you," she admitted at last. "Sit." Turning to Elsie, she frowned. "Why are you just standing about, you lazy girl? Go to the kitchens at once and bring tea and biscuits."

"Your blanket, ma'am," said Elsie, picking it up from a nearby chair.

"I'll do that." Smoothly, Andrew took the blanket from Elsie. "I'm famished – go and get that tea."

Elsie opened her mouth to apologize as Andrew tossed the blanket open over Mrs. Whiston's lap, but when he glanced up over his shoulder, his eyes were dancing. He gave her a wink, and Elsie felt as though a bucket of warm water had been poured over her head. Flustered, she scrambled out of the room, almost tripping over herself on her way out.

She couldn't resist pausing in the hallway as she pulled the door almost closed, peering through the crack. She could hardly believe that such a kind and real creature had really made his way into the cold and heartless manor, but there he was, gently tucking the blanket in around his grandmother's hips. She was muttering and shaking her head, and he laughed off every word she said. Kneeling down, he arranged the blanket around her feet. Mrs. Whiston sat back, looking tired, and Andrew straightened up. He studied her with an expression of warm amusement for a moment, then leaned down and kissed the top of her head.

Elsie wondered where he found such warmth for such a crotchety old woman. Then he turned, and for a moment, looked directly at her. Elsie gasped, grabbed her skirts and ran off down the hall as quickly as she could. But it wasn't just the running that was making her heart beat faster than normal.

CHAPTER 9

Mrs. Whiston had just come back from church – a lengthy and complicated affair, necessitating both her coachmen to help her into the carriage and from the carriage into the church. Elsie was not allowed to accompany her; she was too "scruffy and ordinary", Mrs. Whiston had said, to be seen in public. Instead, Elsie spent the morning fussing over Mrs. Whiston's room and parlor, making sure everything was ready for the old lady's return. The smoother things went when Mrs. Whiston got back, the sooner Elsie could escape and hurry home to see Mama, the highlight of her week.

Now, Elsie could hear the carriage rattling to a halt outside the manor, and she hurried down the hallway to meet Mrs. Whiston at the front door. She could hear her mistress complaining even before she'd opened the big main doors.

"Must you be so cruel?" cried Mrs. Whiston. "Oh, you are so rough. Have you no pity for an old woman who depends on you?"

The coachman's muttered, "Sorry, ma'am," sounded so familiar that Elsie almost giggled. She knew exactly how he felt – but she didn't have much sympathy. At least he only had to deal with the old lady on the odd occasions when she wanted to go somewhere.

"There you are," snapped Mrs. Whiston, spotting Elsie in the doorway. Drops of sweat were running down her paunchy face. "Why are you just standing there, child? Hurry up. Come and help me."

"Yes, ma'am." Elsie ran over and grabbed Mrs. Whiston's arm. "Was the service pleasant?"

"It was much too long," Mrs. Whiston snapped. "That priest just likes to carry on and on. He is so long-winded. And the pews are hard to sit on – could they not furnish us with some cushions? What on earth are they doing with my generous donations into the collection plate?"

Elsie didn't dare to venture her opinion, which was that perhaps they were feeding the poor. She mutely helped Mrs. Whiston into her armchair in the parlor.

"Here you are, ma'am," she said. "I have your tea all ready for you, too." She pointed to the tray, resting on the table beside Mrs. Whiston's chair.

A DAUGHTER'S DESPERATION

Mrs. Whiston glared at her for a few moments. "Very well," she sniffed. "Add an extra lump of sugar for me now. I must have some solace after this dreadful morning."

"Yes, ma'am." Elsie obediently dropped a lump of sugar into the cup with the tongs. She lifted the cup and gave it a gentle stir.

"No." Mrs. Whiston's squawk made Elsie jump so that the cup rattled in the saucer. "What are you doing?"

"I – uh—" Elsie stammered.

"You'll break that cup if you beat the spoon about like that. That is the most priceless china, brought back by my great-uncle from his adventures in Asia – you almost chipped it!" Mrs. Whiston gesticulated angrily. "Have some respect for my valuable things."

"Yes, ma'am. Sorry, ma'am." Elsie quickly put down the spoon and moved to give the cup to Mrs. Whiston, but she was too quick. Mrs. Whiston was still gesturing at the cup and shouting, and as Elsie moved closer to her, the old lady's arm crashed into the saucer. The cup teetered, rattling dangerously. Elsie's heart nearly stopped, and she jolted to stop the teacup from falling. Scalding tea slopped out of the cup and splashed over Elsie's hand, a few drops splattering onto Mrs. Whiston's silken sleeve.

Mrs. Whiston uttered an almost animal howl of horror. "What have you done?"

79

"Oh, ma'am, I'm so sorry," gasped Elsie, putting down the cup and grabbing a napkin. "Let me help you with that." She moved closer to wipe away the few drops of tea, but Mrs. Whiston batted her hand away angrily.

"Stop," she roared. "Don't touch me. Mrs. Corbyn! MRS. CORBYN!"

The housekeeper came running in. "Yes, ma'am?" she said breathlessly.

"Bring me more tea at once," Mrs. Whiston demanded. "And you may as well pay this girl now – I can't bear the sight of her for another moment. Give her three-quarters of her money and send her away. I will suffer her again this evening, but only if she is suitably punished."

A cruel sneer twisted Mrs. Corbyn's features. "With pleasure, ma'am."

"Three quarters?" Elsie's veins felt filled with ice. "But how will I afford my mama's rent and food with only three quarters of my pay?"

Mrs. Whiston's glare was a smoldering thing, a deep and hateful glow from somewhere in the deepest abyss of her throbbing soul. "Don't you dare contradict me," she stated harshly, "or you'll very quickly find that it's halved – or nothing at all."

Tears stung Elsie's eyes.

"Take your money and go," Mrs. Whiston ordered. "I've had more than enough of you for one week."

Elsie's heart ached. She hung her head and nodded mutely, but her heart was weeping. What was she going to tell Mama?

Elsie felt no better that evening as her weary little legs carried her back toward Whiston Manor. Her eyes were fixed on the street in front of her, seeing nothing as she plodded onward. The fading colors of autumn had started to creep into the details of the scene. Her feet crunched on dry leaves, and there was a chill in the air that nipped cruelly at her nose and the tips of her ears. She pulled her shawl a little closer around her shoulders, barely noticing the cold breeze. Her feet were carrying her back to the manor, but her heart was still firmly back in the tenement.

Mama's nose had been red when Elsie got there, her cheeks gray and hollowed with the cold. There were only two tiny piles of coal in the hearth; one had already burned away to almost nothing, its tiny flame a pathetic attempt at warmth. Mama was wrapped in a tattered blanket, huddled listlessly on her sleeping mat. She smiled when Elsie came in but didn't rise.

"Hello, Mama," Elsie said, hurrying to her, trying to hide her worry. "Are you all right?"

"I'm fine, my love," said Mama. "Just tired." Her eyes darted to the pouch clutched in Elsie's hand. "Did you perhaps bring us some dinner?"

Mama was never so direct in asking for food. Elsie's heart felt squeezed by worry. "Yes, Mama, I did," she said. "I brought you some lovely fresh rolls. You'll feel better in no time once you've eaten them."

"Thank you, darling," Mama said.

"Where's Philip?" asked Elsie.

Mama looked away, not answering, as she tore off a piece of the roll in her hands and stuffed it into her mouth.

"Mama?" Elsie asked. "Where is he?"

"I don't know," Mama said, her voice empty and hollow with sadness. "I just don't know, my darling."

In that moment, Elsie had felt like she could strangle her brother. How could he leave Mama alone here in the tenement while he was running around, drinking and causing trouble with his friends? But she hadn't said anything. And now she was doing exactly what he had done – leaving Mama alone all week while she walked back to her warm room and her three meals a day.

She knew that Mama would hardly be able to feed herself on what was left of Elsie's reduced wage once the rent was paid. Elsie was careful to eat nothing while she was there. Angry, she kicked at a pine cone lying in the road. It spun off, rattling across the cobblestones, and skidded into the gutter.

Elsie felt choked by a huge lump in her throat. "I'm sorry, Mama," she whispered to herself. "I just want to be with you." She swallowed, wiping at her damp eyes. "I'm doing my best."

She needed the job to care for Mama, but she still felt like she was betraying her as she reached the manor and entered it through the servants' entrance. Inside, fires throughout the house had warmed the air; Elsie pulled off her shawl as she walked up to her room. She wondered if Mrs. Whiston had forgiven her yet, or at least forgotten about that morning's incident with the tea.

As Elsie quickly put away her shawl and coat in her room, she could hear voices from the parlor down the hall. One, high-pitched and irritable as always, was Mrs. Whiston's. Elsie groaned inwardly as she left her room and headed toward her mistress's voice. She didn't feel like waiting hand and foot on the old lady now; she was always so much more demanding when she had visitors, and the visitors sometimes seemed to think that they could order Elsie around, too.

As she turned the corner in the passage, she suddenly recognized the second voice. It was soft and lilting, sounding vaguely amused in its musical quality, and it inexplicably made her heart beat faster. Her step quickened. *Andrew.*

When she cracked the door open, he was sitting on the settee with his back to her, listening as Mrs. Whiston told one of her long and rambling stories. As Elsie entered, Andrew turned to look at her. Their eyes met for a moment, and Andrew smiled. The expression was warm sunshine on her frozen, frightened heart.

"Hello," Elsie mouthed, knowing that speaking aloud to Andrew was sure to get her into trouble. He gave her a tiny nod, then turned back to Mrs. Whiston. "And then what happened?" he asked.

Mrs. Whiston paused to give Elsie her standard cold glare, then went on. "Well, I was deep in conversation with the Baroness of Guernsey, and so I didn't notice at first how terrible Mrs. Abbott's stew truly was. The Baroness was a most interesting person, Andrew. A most distinguished and gentle lady with impeccable taste…"

Elsie had long since stopped listening to Mrs. Whiston's long-winded stories. She set about her business of poking the fire, arranging Mrs. Whiston's lap-blanket, and obeying the hundreds of little demands that she peppered about seemingly just to keep Elsie busy.

Finally, the story came to an end, and Andrew laughed politely. "That's terrible, Grandmother," he said.

"Isn't it? You would think that a doctor's wife would have better staff – and know how stew should actually taste." Mrs. Whiston sniffed. "I suppose not everyone has a distinguished and delicate palate like mine."

"How have you been, otherwise?" asked Andrew.

"Terrible, I'm afraid, my boy," said Mrs. Whiston. "I am surrounded by the most incompetent staff. You would not believe how badly that coachman drove me to church this morning – it felt as though he was taking the carriage over every bump in the road."

"I'm sure that's not the case," said Andrew mildly.

"And *this* girl." Mrs. Whiston shook her head as if she were bearing some great burden. "She spilled my tea on me this morning. The whole cup, all over me – it was most painful. I reduced her pay, but I think I should probably have dismissed her."

Elsie gave Andrew a desperate look. His eyes met hers and studied her seriously for a moment, a look of pity filling his eyes. Turning back to his grandmother, he spoke gently. "I'm sure it was just a mistake, Grandmother. I've seen that Elsie takes excellent care of you. Don't you think that reducing her pay for such a small incident was a little harsh?"

Startled, Elsie stared at him. She couldn't utter a word. What was this? How did Andrew even know her name?

Mrs. Whiston frowned. "Don't be ridiculous, Andrew. What do you know of such matters?" She patted his hand. "Leave it to me, child. Don't worry about such things. If she continues to prove utterly useless, I will dismiss her without further ado."

After a few minutes' polite conversation, Andrew rose. "Please excuse me for a moment, Grandmother. I would like to use the lavatory."

Mrs. Whiston raised a dismissive hand. "As you wish, child."

"You, girl." Andrew nodded toward Elsie. "Fetch us some more tea, if you please."

Elsie lowered her head. "Yes, sir."

She followed the older boy out of the room, her eyes fixed on her feet. She felt a little flustered, unable to understand why Andrew had stuck up for her the way he did. About to hurry off to the kitchen, she was stopped when he reached out, touching her arm with the lightest brush of his fingertips.

Startled, Elsie stopped, looking up at him. His eyes were gentle and filled with regret.

"I'm sorry about my grandmother," he said.

"Sir?" Elsie stammered.

"Oh, you know what I mean. She can be such a grumpy old bat," Andrew said. "I don't think it was right of her to cut your pay – but there's no convincing her once she's made up her mind." He grimaced. "I'm sorry."

"N-no, sir. It's all right," Elsie said.

"It isn't really, and I know it." Andrew sighed. "There's not much to be done, I'm afraid. She's so set in her ways, we'll never change her."

Elsie couldn't believe the young master was speaking to her so plainly. She simply lowered her eyes and nodded. There was a moment of awkward silence, and then he said, "You're taking good care of her, you know. Thank you. I do love the old crone, even if she is rather a bore."

"Thank you, sir," whispered Elsie.

"I guess you'd better run along now." Andrew smiled. "Don't let her get under your skin, though, all right? It's not personal. It's just how she is."

Elsie nodded and hurried off toward the kitchens, her heart hammering so loudly that she feared Andrew might hear it all the way back in the hallway.

PART II

CHAPTER 10

Two Years Later

Mrs. Whiston's face was purple with effort. She painstakingly pinned down her mutton with her fork, her hand trembling violently. Lips pursed in concentration, she worked her knife backward and forward across it, a monumental effort of jerky strokes that achieved little.

"Here, ma'am." Elsie stepped closer from her customary place behind Mrs. Whiston's chair at the dining table. "Allow me."

Mrs. Whiston fell back in her chair, exhausted. She gave Elsie an angry glance but didn't protest as Elsie pried the knife and fork from the old lady's hands and quickly cut up her meat. Elsie's own stomach rumbled as the heavenly scent of the mutton rose into the air. She hadn't had a chance to eat anything yet today – Mrs. Whiston had been particularly demanding, sending Elsie scurrying this way and that all morning.

Not that this was a new occurrence for Elsie. Two years of caring for Mrs. Whiston had continued at a monotonous pace—the only thing that changed was that Mrs. Whiston grew all the more demanding the older she became.

"There you are," said Elsie, handing Mrs. Whiston's fork back to her.

"Don't patronize me," snapped Mrs. Whiston, grabbing the fork. "I could do all this for myself, you know, if I was so inclined."

"Of course, you could, ma'am," said Elsie soothingly.

"Are you mocking me?" Mrs. Whiston glared at her with her piggy eyes from deep in her pasty face.

"Not at all, ma'am. I wouldn't dare," Elsie placated her.

Mrs. Whiston grumbled, turning back to her lunch. Elsie poured some more gravy over her mutton before being asked and watched as the old lady fed herself in shaky little gulps. Her stomach rumbled, and she hoped that Mrs. Whiston couldn't hear.

Mrs. Whiston looked up from her mashed potatoes and glared at Elsie. "What are you staring at?" she demanded.

A DAUGHTER'S DESPERATION

"Does it amuse you to see a helpless old woman struggling with the most basic of tasks?"

"No, ma'am," said Elsie. "I was merely waiting to see if you needed anything more."

"Of course, I need something more," Mrs. Whiston spluttered, lightly spraying her plate with drops of gravy. "Can't you see that there are not nearly enough vegetables on this plate? Fetch me more at once."

"They're right here, ma'am," said Elsie. She rose and picked up the tureen of roast vegetables from the middle of the table, spooning some more onto Mrs. Whiston's plate. To Elsie's relief, the old lady stuffed her mouth with another forkful of food and masticated it vigorously, her chin wobbling as she tucked in. Elsie quietly resumed her place behind Mrs. Whiston's chair.

She tried to tell herself that Mrs. Whiston's words didn't sting her anymore. She had gotten so used to them and tried to respond always with nothing but kindness. Yet still, even two years later, they still chafed.

After a few minutes' grumbling as she ate, Mrs. Whiston laid down her knife and fork. "I'm tired," she said simply. "Take me to my chambers."

With the aid of a sturdy walking stick and plenty of help from Elsie, Mrs. Whiston hoisted herself from her chair, shuffled down the hallway, and stood propped up in the corner while

Elsie turned the covers of her sumptuous bed. Finally, she succeeded in getting Mrs. Whiston into the bed and tucking her in—since the woman napped in her regular gown.

The old lady fussed and complained; nothing Elsie did was right – she pulled the sheet up too high, then she tucked in the comforter too tightly, then she was supposed to have plumped up the pillows before turning the covers, which necessitated extricating Mrs. Whiston from the bed and repeating the entire performance all over again. At last, the old lady was suitably composed, and Elsie waited to hear the first gentle snore before slipping quietly out of the room.

Mrs. Whiston would nap for about thirty-five minutes, as was her habit. Until she awoke – and she would be irate when she did, shouting for her afternoon tea – Elsie had a rare moment of freedom, and she gripped it with both hands.

The big house was silent as Elsie wandered down the corridors. Her room had started to feel tiny and cramped; instead, she directed her steps outside, to where summer blazed in all its glory among the meticulous gardens and the stately orchard. She wondered why Mrs. Whiston spent all her time fussing and complaining among her dusty old treasures and heirlooms too expensive to touch or enjoy. There was a world of priceless beauty just outside the manor – a beauty so timeless that it could not be purchased or plundered or even manufactured; a beauty that grew up from the very earth and blessed all, freely, with its abundance.

Stepping out of the servants' entrance and into the back of the garden, Elsie took a deep breath. The scents of the flowers in the garden rose up to greet her, softly touching her senses with their sweetness. She smiled. Even though Mrs. Whiston didn't seem to have much time for the garden, at least Elsie could appreciate it. She strolled slowly across the lawn, enjoying the shady hedges and the neatly pruned trees that lined the footpath, before making her way into the orchard.

As magical as the canopy had always looked to her from her bedroom window, the orchard was even more beautiful inside. She walked slowly, listening to the soft rush of the breeze in the rich branches. The dappled shade was a relief after the warm sun; the fruity smells of peach and apple trees lightly touched the air, and the deep green grass was soft and cool on Elsie's bare feet. She reached out her hands as she walked, allowing her fingertips to brush against the rough bark of the tree trunks. Gnarled as they were, these trees were as old as they were lovely, and Elsie knew them like old friends.

There was a bright, musical twitter from a nearby branch, and Elsie looked up to see her old friend, the little robin, perched on a twig. It studied her with its bright button eyes, then flitted to the ground at her feet, hopping across the grass and giving demanding little chirps.

"Of course, I do," Elsie laughed. She reached into her apron pocket and scattered some breadcrumbs on the grass. "I wouldn't forget about your lunch, my little friend."

The robin gave a contented chirp and started to peck at the breadcrumbs. Elsie headed onward, aware that the robin was flitting from branch to branch beside her. Ahead, between the trees, she could see the whitewashed wall of the cottage.

The robin chirped.

"I know," said Elsie. "It's silly of me to keep coming to this little cottage – and yet something about it just draws me."

She had reached the front door, and she stared up at it, admiring the homey little building. It squatted comfortably among the trees, the boards over its windows making it look sleepy, its fat chimney cold and empty where it sprouted from a thatched roof. She could tell that the cottage wasn't horribly old and still was in good condition – much better than Mama's tenement – but it had the cold feel of a place that had been empty for a long, long time. Cautiously, Elsie pushed the front door open and stepped inside. She'd never dared to before.

There were no furnishings in the cottage except for a layer of dust on the windowsills and the silvery shadows of cobwebs in all the corners. Elsie sighed as she stepped inside, gazing around at what must have been the kitchen, once. Closing her eyes, she started to imagine furnishings for the cottage, describing them to the robin, which sat on a tree branch just outside the door.

"Some beautiful oak cupboards over here," she said, gesturing to the kitchen wall. "With the kitchen sink right beneath that window, so that I can stand here and do the dishes and watch the animals and birds in the orchard. A kitchen table here, set with five places – for my three children, and for me, and for... you know." She glanced back at the open door. "It's too silly to say aloud, but it's my dream. Let me dream it."

The robin uttered an agreeing twitter.

"Checkered red curtains on the kitchen windows." Elsie turned slowly, her arms spread out, dreaming. "A fire blazing in the fireplace, and a great thick hearth-rug where the children can play in the evenings." She headed out of the kitchen and into the living room. "Soft sofas here," she murmured, "deeply padded, where one could snuggle down and read for hours in the cold winter." Ascending the stairs, she reached the bedrooms. "This little room for my little boy, Peter," she said, "and the bigger one for the two girls – Catherine and Hattie." Her steps slowed as she continued down the hallway, her feet ringing on the wooden floor. "And here," she whispered, pushing open the door to the larger bedroom, "this is our room."

She peered through the window and saw the robin fluttering on the branch. He contented himself with fluffing up his feathers. Elsie went to stand in the middle of the floor, gazing around the empty little room. "A dresser right there," she said. "A wardrobe here. A lace curtain here. And here, our bed." She sighed, closing her eyes. "It's so cold in this room alone, Robin," she continued talking to the bird, although surely it could no longer hear her. "I just can't help missing Mama's arms tucked around me, holding me when things get hard." She blinked back tears. "I can't wait to one day lie warm and safe in the arms of a man who loves me."

Heading to the window again, she knocked on the pane of glass, startling the robin. It flew off to a higher perch. Elsie leaned her elbows on the window sill and gazed toward the main house, wishing that a certain tall, elegant figure would come around the corner toward her.

"Safe in Andrew's arms," she whispered.

CHAPTER 11

As Elsie walked down the dirty streets of Whitechapel toward her a visit with her mother, she couldn't help imagining the cottage as she had pictured it. Her thin soles squelched in the mud and nameless dirt clung to her shoes with every step. She tried not to think of how terrible she was going to smell by the time she returned the manor again. Instead, she quickened her step, looking up eagerly for the tenement house.

Some of the old houses around her had simply fallen apart in the past two years. One was just a heap of rubble now, bits of its frame still extending shaky fingers up into the sky, its guts a mere pile of disintegrated building material on the floor. Rats squeaked and disappeared into nooks and crannies as Elsie walked past.

Her mother's tenement building, however, like many others,

was still standing despite its advancing decrepitude. Looking up, Elsie could see that yet another roof tile had blown free and disappeared somewhere into the chaos of the streets. She carefully opened the sagging front door, propping it up with her shoulder to prevent it from crashing off its remaining hinge, and proceeded down the corridor. The smell of mold was overwhelming.

"Mama," Elsie called out, reaching for the tenement door and opening it. "I'm here!"

"Elsie. At last."

Mama was kneeling by the fire, poking sticks of firewood underneath a pot that straddled the weak flames. Elsie could tell by the smell that nothing was boiling in there except water. She put her cloth bag down on the table. "I brought you some beets and turnips, Mama," she said. "And even a little bit of tripe."

"Thank you, love," said Mama, not looking up from the fire.

Elsie stood by the table, studying her mother, a hint of nervousness starting to seep into her heart. Why was Mama not getting up to greet her?

"Mama, how are you feeling?" she asked.

"Darling, would you do something for me?"

"Of course. Anything." Elsie's heart pounded. What was wrong?

"Be a dear and rinse those plates in the bucket." Mama pointed to the two dirty plates on the table. "Then I'll get the vegetables and tripe started."

"Yes, Mama," said Elsie, obediently. She picked up the plates. "Where's the other one?"

"You don't need to bring a third plate," said Mama curtly.

Elsie decided against asking why not but worry gripped her. Again, where was Philip? What was Mama not telling her? Nervously, she swilled the plates around in the bucket of semi-clean water standing in the corner. Even some industrious scrubbing with a rag couldn't remove the oily slick from their surface. Elsie did her best, drying them with a ragged cloth, and set them on the table. Mama was stirring the pot of food, and Elsie saw that she was staring anxiously at the meager coal. She didn't know if it was going to be enough.

"Here, Mama." Elsie stepped closer, reaching for the wooden spoon. "Let me do this. Why don't you sit down? You look tired."

"Thank you, love." Mama still didn't look at Elsie or embrace her. She shuffled off and sat down on her sleeping mat, hugging her knees to her chest. Her eyes gazed straight into the fire, and Elsie noticed that her face was paler than ever. She seemed to be making an effort to force out every breath, her cheeks puffing as she fought to move the air.

Elsie held down her worry, cooking the dinner as quickly as she could and spooning it out onto her mother's plate. Bringing the food over to the sleeping mat, she crouched beside Mama and held out the plate. "Here you go," she said softly.

"I'm honestly not that hungry."

"Mama, you must eat." Elsie forced a spoon into Mama's right hand and the plate into her left. "You need to get your strength up."

"And you? You're not eating?"

"I ate at the manor before I left," she lied.

Sighing, Mama began to eat, blowing on the hot spoonfuls of the watery stew. Elsie waited until she had taken a few bites before speaking gently. "Mama, where's Philip?"

Mama's face crumpled. Her wrinkles deepened as an expression of agony filled her face, and she squeezed her eyes tight shut, the corners of her mouth trembling. A single sob clutched at her throat before she shook it off and managed to squeeze out the words. "Elsie, I didn't want to tell you—your burden is heavy enough. B-but your brother's been arrested."

"Arrested?" Elsie gasped. "What for? What's happened? Where is he now?"

"I don't know. I happened way last Monday," Mama cried. "Mrs. Davies next door came and told me that she saw our

Philip and her son and some of their friends running through the streets as fast as they could with the police right behind them. She sent her younger boy to follow them right away and see what happened, and oh—"

Mama paused, choking back her tears. "Oh, Elsie, they caught them, *all* of them. They took my boy away with his hands bound." A single tear escaped and ran down Mama's cheeks, getting lost and soaked into the maze of wrinkles. "They've arrested him, Elsie. I don't know what he's done. And I don't know where they took him. A messenger just brought me a letter Friday afternoon saying that Phillip will stand trial on Tuesday, and there's nobody to help him." She swallowed. "I don't know what to do. I've been worried sick all week."

Elsie's heart sank, yet she could find no surprise in her mind for what her mother had just told her.

"I'm so sorry," she said. "We've had so many arguments with Philip. I worried he was going to get in trouble. And now he has." Elsie felt sick to her stomach. "He wouldn't listen to you, Mama. You know what he's like. He wouldn't listen."

"I know." Mama wiped away a tear. "Elsie, how are we going to help him now?"

Staring at her mother, Elsie had to swallow back a sudden wave of anger and hatred. Philip was supposed to be taking care of Mama. If he would just earn an honest living, he could make sure that Mama had enough to eat, perhaps move her to a better tenement or even get her some help from a doctor.

Instead, he was doing nothing except making their mother worry.

"Mama, you're not well." Elsie put an arm around her mother's shoulders. "It won't do you any good to get upset about this."

"I have to be at the trial," gasped Mama. "How am I going to get to the courthouse? How will I make it back home?"

"Hush, now." Elsie pulled Mama closer. "Shhh. Don't worry about a thing, Mama. You won't have to go to the trial."

"But we must know what happens. If no one is there…"

"I will go." Elsie kissed the top of Mama's head. "I'm going to be there for him."

"You?" Mama stared at her. "It's a Tuesday, Elsie. You have to work."

"I'm sure Mrs. Whiston will let me off under the circumstances," said Elsie, knowing full well the old lady would *never* let that happen, and also knowing that she would have to make some kind of a plan if she wanted to help both her brother and her mother. "Don't worry, Mama. I'll be there. I'll take care of him – I promise."

"Oh, Elsie." Mama stared at her, her eyes sparkling with tears. "But who will take care of you?"

Elsie paused. Unexpectedly, her mind filled with the image of Andrew, his gentle face, his crooked smile, his compassionate voice, and she felt safer than she had ever felt.

"Maybe someone will, Mama," she said. "Don't you worry. Somebody will."

※

"No, not like that!" Mrs. Whiston complained. "You can't do it like that. How do you expect a fire ever to warm the house if you build it like that?"

"I'm sure she knows what she's doing, Grandmother," said Andrew with a bemused smile. He glanced over at Elsie, who knelt on the hearth-rug, scooping some more coal into the fire. She smiled back, and Andrew gave his head a tiny shake of exasperation.

"Knows what she's doing?" demanded Mrs. Whiston. "How would she possibly know what she's doing?"

"Well, she has been your maid for two years," Andrew pointed out calmly.

"And still she's learned nothing in all that time," snapped Mrs. Whiston. "Can you imagine working for so long and having no idea how to do your job?"

"Oh, I'm sure it's not so bad," said Andrew.

"You don't have to live with her every day," said Mrs. Whiston. "Do you know how dreadful this girl's hands are? If they're not too cold, they're too hot. She all but kills me helping me into my clothes every morning, I tell you."

Elsie looked over at Andrew and gave him a tiny shrug. She saw him sigh, but he smiled at his grandmother. "Don't let that upset you just now, Grandmother," he said pleasantly. "You were telling me about Grandfather's ships, weren't you?"

The old lady grumbled a little more, smoothing out her blanket, but Andrew seemed to have succeeded in placating her.

"Yes, yes," she said impatiently. "One of them was damaged in a storm off the coast of Africa, but they managed to repair it, and now it's on its way to India. Another is going to that dreadful new continent full of savages, but I'll be surprised if it comes back. I'm quite certain that all of the sailors will be murdered by those uncultured barbarians the moment that it reaches the shore."

"Actually, Grandmother, quite a few sources have said that the native people of the New World are quite peaceful," said Andrew.

"Peaceful? My dear, they run around wearing loincloths and spearing animals," said Grandmother disdainfully. "I don't think they'd know the word *peace* if you spelled it out for them."

Elsie took up her place behind Mrs. Whiston's chair and gave Andrew a smile, inclining her head. *Thank you for rescuing me back there.*

Between the two of them, a glance could say everything. Andrew returned it with a pleased look from hooded eyes. *It's my pleasure.*

Mrs. Whiston continued to waffle on about ships, pirates, savages and slaves for what seemed like hours. Elsie wasn't listening; instead, she worried about Philip. He must have spent last night in a cell. Was he safe? Was it cold there? And what about tomorrow's trial? She had told Mama that she would be there, but she had no idea how. A few times she had to swallow back tears as she stood behind Mrs. Whiston's chair.

Elsie's feet were aching when, finally, Mrs. Whiston raised her hands into her lap. "I am quite exhausted," she said. "You know, Andrew, it really is cruel of you to stay so long. This late hour is truly disagreeable for an old lady in my condition."

"I apologize for inconveniencing you then, Grandmother," said Andrew, getting up. He gave Elsie a wry look, and she returned it with a tiny shrug, although her mind was almost too far away to notice. "Would you like to go to bed?"

"What do you think? I just said that I'm exhausted," said Mrs. Whiston. "Come on, girl. Do what I pay you to do and get me to bed."

Elsie refrained from commenting that Mrs. Whiston barely paid her at all. She helped the old lady to her feet and supported her toward her bedchamber, enduring more complaining and fussing as Mrs. Whiston undressed and was escorted into bed. Elsie arranged her covers and pillows exactly the way that she wanted, attended to a thousand little needs, and finally blew out the lamp. Mrs. Whiston was snoring before Elsie could leave the room.

Elsie wasn't surprised to see Andrew standing in the hallway. He often waited for her after Mrs. Whiston had gone to bed, hoping to exchange a few words before he had to leave.

"She was especially difficult today, wasn't she?" he said softly, his gentle eyes studying her as she closed the door behind her.

"Oh, it's nothing new," said Elsie with a smile. "You know her – she's never happy unless she's unhappy."

Andrew laughed. "That's true. Well, at least you can say this for my grandmother – she's consistently a miserable old bat."

"And getting increasingly more miserable as she ages," Elsie agreed.

Andrew laughed. "Well, the older she gets, the more practice she's had."

They walked slowly down the hallway. Elsie knew that Andrew would leave soon, but she wished that she could ask him to stay. She glanced down at his hand, hanging loosely by his side, and felt a sudden urge to reach out and take his fingers in hers. Surprised at herself, she buried her hands in her apron pockets.

"What is the matter?" Andrew asked softly.

She looked up, startled. "No, nothing," she said quickly. *Has he read my mind?* "My – my hands are just cold," she stammered.

He gave her a dubious look, and Elsie immediately felt stupid in the warm summer air.

"You've been quiet all evening," said Andrew. "Well, I know that you're always quiet, considering that my grandmother jumps down your throat every time you open your mouth. But still – it feels as though something is weighing on you." They had reached the entrance hall, and Andrew turned to face her. The lamplight made his eyes seem even deeper, gentleness making his voice more pleasant than ever. "What is it, Elsie?"

Elsie looked away. She knew that she should just respond with, "All is well, sir," and bid Andrew good night. Yet something was always drawing her closer and closer to him, urging her to tell him more, to get nearer to him. She could not resist.

"It's my brother," she whispered at last. "Philip."

"What's happened?" asked Andrew. He reached out, laying a hand on her shoulder, and his touch made her entire body tingle. "Is he all right?"

"No." Tears choked Elsie's eyes and throat. She swallowed them back, forcing the words out. "He's been arrested, and he's standing trial tomorrow. I don't know what he's done." She sniffed. "He's going to be alone, Andrew. And we shan't know what's happened to him."

She saw Andrew's jaw tense. "And your mother is too sick to leave the tenement."

Elsie nodded. "And my father is long gone."

Andrew sighed, and his grip tightened on Elsie's shoulder. "You can't let him be alone, Elsie."

"I know. I told my mama I would be there," said Elsie. "But what can I do?"

"You can go." Andrew touched her chin with a finger, lifting it so that he could look into her eyes, his gaze searching hers. "Go and be there for your brother."

"What about Mrs. Whiston?" whispered Elsie. "I can't lose this job, Andrew."

"I know that," said Andrew. "That's why I'm going to stay here and cover for you."

Elsie's eyes filled with tears. "You would do that for me?"

"Elsie Griggs." Andrew leaned closer, and for a moment that seemed to last far too long and far too short at the same time, he pressed his lips to the top of her head. "When will you realize that I would do anything for you?"

Then he was gone. Elsie's skin burned where he had kissed her, setting every cell in her body on fire.

CHAPTER 12

Elsie's neck ached from straining to see over the large crowd that had gathered around the courthouse. It had taken her and Andrew longer than expected to sneak her out of the manor without Mrs. Whiston noticing. Now, she had only been able to find a place right in the back of the room.

There were four prisoners standing in the dock, their heads hanging, and Elsie had to stand on tiptoe to spot Philip. He was in the corner of the dock, and Elsie hated the way he looked. She had expected her brother to be defiant, to be glaring up at the judge with the same stubborn pride that was forever getting him into trouble. Instead, his shoulders were slumped, his eyes staring fixedly at the wooden floor between his scuffed and broken shoes. He didn't look defiant. He looked defeated, and it scared her.

"Come on, Philip," she whispered. "Say something. You've got to be innocent."

The day had worn on for hours. Elsie couldn't see out of the high windows of the courtroom, but the air had a sleepy, late afternoon feeling to it. Her aching feet told her that she'd been waiting for a long time, and she wished that she'd understood more of the proceedings. Witnesses had spoken about the events in question, each of their stories sounding different to Elsie; the policemen had talked at length, and two stern men that the others addressed as "solicitor" had been asking lots of questions.

All Elsie really knew was that the broad, fat man sitting at the very top of the room – his powdered wig tumbling majestically onto his powerful shoulders – was the judge. And that when he tapped his wooden hammer, Philip's fate would be decided.

They had questioned Philip, too, both of the solicitors. They had sounded angry, and Philip's answers had been muttered monotones. Elsie wished she could run up to him and shout at him. Slap him. Tell him that he had to fight back – that he had to prove his innocence, whether he really was innocent or not—and she knew that he most likely was not. She didn't care. She needed him to be set free again, so that he could help her to care for Mama. Anger rose in her throat, and Elsie had to choke it down like bile. How could Philip betray them like this?

There was a commotion from somewhere outside the courtroom. Elsie looked up to see that the men were making their way back into the room, and one glance at their expressions made worry twist in her stomach. They wore grim, bitter looks of determination, and Elsie's breath caught in her throat. She looked over at Philip. He was staring at the men, too, and for the first time in years, Elsie knew exactly the look on his face. It was fear – raw fear.

"Oh, Philip," Elsie whispered. "Oh, please, Philip, let them set you free."

Her anger melted away, and she wanted to run to him and put her arms around him like she had done when they were both little children. But right now, there was nothing she could do except watch as the men took their places once more.

One man stepped out from the benches and walked up to the judge. There was a hushed exchange, and a piece of paper was handed up to the judge. Ponderously putting on a pair of small, round spectacles, the judge inspected it, and Elsie realized that she'd crossed all of her fingers.

"Please," she whispered. "Please, let Philip be set free." Her stomach churned, and she held her breath as the judge looked back up.

The judge cleared his throat. "The court has reached a decision," he said pompously. "All of the prisoners are hereby found to be guilty of the charges, namely, robbing Mr.

Albertus Finch and assaulting him with the intent to do grievous bodily harm."

Elsie's breath caught. Guilty? How would Philip be punished? She couldn't bear to look over at the victim, who sat in the bench wearing a satisfied expression.

"The prisoners are sentenced as follows." The judge peered at the paper. "Mr. Patrick Harris will be transported to serve three years of labor in the penal colonies of Australia."

Elsie swallowed, her hands shaking, sudden hope clutching at her. Her brother might just escape the death penalty – but to serve in the penal colonies was hardly any better. Nobody ever came back from Australia, even if they survived the years of unpaid labor.

"Mr. Jason Price," the judge continued. "Two years of labor in the penal colonies of Australia…"

Elsie watched the judge read further and further down the list. She knew that Philip was staring at him, too, but in that moment, she couldn't bear to look over at her brother. She couldn't imagine the fear that must be filling him now; it had to be akin to the terror that was now gripping her own heart, sucking at her stomach.

"Mr. Philip Griggs," the judge read at last. He paused, glancing severely over his spectacles. "As the ringleader of the gang that assaulted Mr. Finch, you will be sentenced to five years of labor in the penal colonies." With that, the judge slapped the paper down on his bench, raised the gavel and rapped it sharply. The sound was flat and final. "This court is now adjourned."

Elsie felt as though she couldn't breathe. Five *years* in Australia, and even if Philip survived, he would never be able to find his way back home – not without any money. He was going away. He was going away forever, and Elsie knew, with sudden terror, that she would never see her brother again.

Only then did she look at him. Already the prison guards were herding him out of the docks, but he was standing stock-still, staring up at the bench as if he couldn't believe what he'd just heard. His mouth hung open, and his eyes were stretched wide with regret.

Elsie wanted to scream out his name. She wanted to run and grab him in her arms and let nobody take him away. But instead she stood frozen, staring at him, until the prison guard grabbed his arm and he was dragged away. He did not look up. He did not see her.

And then, he was gone.

THE WALK BACK TO THE TENEMENT BUILDING HAD NEVER felt so long, yet in the same breath, so far from long enough. Elsie dragged her feet, not caring that the foul-smelling mud of the slum streets was splattering against the hem of her worn dress. It was too short now, anyway, but at the moment, Elsie couldn't bring herself to care. She couldn't care about anything except the tremendous weight of pain and worry that was dragging on her heart.

Philip was gone. She could hardly believe it. And, worse, how would Mama take it? How was she going to tell her mother that Philip really had assaulted and robbed a man, and that as punishment for that crime, he was going to be taken away from everything he'd ever known? Taken away from her, who had never done anything except love him as her little boy, even when he'd strayed from everything she'd ever taught him?

She reached the tenement building, but for the first time, Elsie didn't want to go inside and face her mother. She had no idea how she was going to tell Mama what had just happened. But standing outside would achieve nothing, so after a few long moments, she directed her reluctant steps into the building.

Mama was sitting on her sleeping mat when Elsie came in, and for a moment, she thought that her mother was asleep. Then she saw the dress spread over Mama's knees and the needle in her hand. Leaning closer to the fire in order to see better, Mama was trying to work a patch onto the dress, but Elsie could see that her hands were trembling.

"Mama?" she said softly.

Mama looked up, and her eyes were lined with worry. "My

dear!" She set the dress aside and struggled to her feet, her movement slow and painful. "You made it to the trial?" Her eyes filled with tears. "How did you do it?"

"I had some help from a friend," said Elsie softly, embracing her mother. "What are you doing?"

"Some mending," said Mama with a courageous smile. "It brings in a few pennies, at least."

Staring into Mama's eyes, Elsie realized then that Mama knew. She hadn't been at the trial, but she knew that her son was guilty. She knew that she had to make do without him now. She knew that she was never going to see him again, and even though she knew, there was still a whisper of hope in her sunken eyes.

"So," Mama prompted. "How did the trial go?"

The end of the sentence turned up with a hint of faith, and Elsie knew that she couldn't tell her. If she told Mama that her worst fears had been realized, it would break her. She would collapse where she stood and die of a broken heart, and Elsie didn't think she could bear it.

"It – it was all right," Elsie stammered out, her mind spinning as she grasped for a plausible answer. "It went all right. They..." She paused, grappling with herself. Could she really lie to her mother? Then again, could she really inflict the appalling truth on her? "They were still deciding," she said at last, her stomach twisting with the lie. "I didn't quite catch what they wanted to do. I'll go back tomorrow and find out."

Mama studied her for a moment, a flicker of uncertainty in her eyes. Elsie bit her lip, terrified that Mama was going to suspect her of lying. Instead, she looked away with a sad smile. "Thank you, darling," she said. "I would appreciate that, if you can get away."

Elsie didn't know what to say. She moved over to the kitchen cupboards and started opening them. "I need to get back to work, but can I start a soup or something for you?" she asked.

"That would be nice," said Mama. Elsie heard the sleeping mat rustle as Mama sat down and picked up the dress she'd been mending. She opened a cupboard and found a single carrot and a slightly moldy potato on the shelf, and her stomach twisted with nausea. Was this really all that Mama had left to survive the week?

"I still have a little money," Mama said quickly. "I'll go and get some more to eat for the rest of the week tomorrow." She raised the dress she was holding with a sheepish smile. "I just want to get this done first."

Elsie stared at her, realizing that perhaps she wasn't the only person who'd told a white lie today.

There was a loud banging on the door. Elsie jumped and looked at Mama. "Are you expecting someone?" she asked.

Mama's eyes grew large. She blinked rapidly and Elsie got a horrible feeling in her gut. The banging came again.

"I knew you're in there!" the voice bellowed through the door.

"Mr. Jameson," Elsie cried, recognizing his voice. "Mama, it's not time for the rent. We have another five days yet."

Mama wouldn't meet her eyes.

"What's happened?" Elsie asked, her heart sinking to her feet.

The banging grew louder. "Open up! You'll be out on the streets!" he shouted.

Elsie went to the door and opened it just as Mr. Jameson was going to pound again. He nearly struck her in the face.

"About time," he ground out through yellowed teeth. "Where's the rest of the rent?"

Elsie involuntarily took a step back. "We paid, Mr. Jameson. We always pay on time, you know that."

He glared at Mama. "Your boy didn't pay the full amount."

Mama sucked in her breath and reached slowly under her sleeping pallet. She pulled out a few coins which Elsie knew were Mama's food money. Elsie reluctantly took them and held them out to the man whose stomach hung over his pants like an extra appendage.

"Is this enough?"

He snatched the money from her and counted it out begrudgingly. He gave what could only be termed a growl and stepped back into the hallway. "See you're not short again," he ordered gruffly, slamming their door behind him.

"Mama?" Elsie asked, trying to control her trembling.

"Philip... He was to pay..."

"H-he must have counted wrong," Elsie said, trying to ease the sorrow on her mother's face. How dare her brother! How dare he! For a brief moment, she was glad he was being shipped to the other side of the world, but the feeling was short-lived. Even with all his faults, he was needed. Sometimes, he brought food, and Elsie knew his presence was a comfort to Mama.

"It's all right," Mama said stoically. "You're making me food right now. It'll last me just fine. I didn't need that money."

"You do need it," Elsie said. "But I'll bring you extra food next time. I promise."

And she would. But what was Mama going to without Philip? What were they both going to do?

CHAPTER 13

The cook had long since given over the task of making the old lady's tea to Elsie. In truth, Elsie didn't mind—it gave her an excuse to be away from the woman a bit longer. Now, the kettle whistled, a shrill sound puffing out on a cloud of steam. For once, Elsie didn't jump up to grab it. Instead, her movements were slow and sluggish as she poured the tea. She gazed listlessly into the fine china cup as the rich liquid swirled around inside it. She knew that Mrs. Whiston was going to shout at her when she arrived with the tea, but Mrs. Whiston was going to shout anyway. What was the point in hurrying? Especially today, when her heart felt so heavy that she staggered under the unrelenting weight of it.

She dropped two sugar cubes into the cup and slowly stirred the tea, sighing inwardly. Her hands were busy with the tea, but her heart was torn in two – one half in the tenement where Mama was cold and starving, the other half on a ship going to Australia with her brother. Did he regret what he'd done? Did he wish, now, that he'd heeded Mama's warnings? Or had the punishment only made him even more angry?

"Elsie?"

The voice startled her so badly that she dropped the teaspoon. It clattered to the ground, bouncing and tumbling over the flagstones of the kitchen floor. Elsie spun around to find Andrew standing directly behind her, only a couple of feet from her. The scent of him enveloped her, making her heart hammer even faster. He was so close that she could see the faint dusting of hair on his upper lip, the depth of the worry in his dark green eyes.

"Andrew." Her voice was breathless.

"I'm sorry. I didn't mean to startle you," said Andrew, smiling. Elsie felt the warmth of the smile to the very bottom of her toes. "I called out as I came in, but you seemed to be very deep in thought."

Elsie felt her face heating up with the force of a blush. She ducked, quickly fishing the teaspoon up from the floor. "I – that's no trouble." She swallowed, realizing that in her fright, she'd called him by his first name. She hoped the sneaky little chambermaids weren't listening in on their conversation. Putting the spoon in the sink, she grabbed a new one and quickly laid it out on the tray with Mrs. Whiston's tea. "I'm sorry to have ignored you. I-I should be getting this to your grandmother."

"She can wait for a moment." Andrew laid a hand on Elsie's shoulder, and his touch sent a jolt of warmth through her entire being. "First tell me, how did the trial go yesterday?"

Absurdly, Elsie felt her eyes filling with tears. She screwed them tightly shut, trying to hold the tears back, but they leaked out from beneath her lashes and spilled hot and wet down her cheeks. A sob gripped her throat, and she had to choke it down with a deep breath.

"Elsie?" Andrew's grip tightened on her shoulder, worry filling his voice. "What's the matter? What happened?"

"They sent him to Australia, Andrew." Elsie sniffed, hearing her voice crack. "They sent my brother to Australia for *five years*."

"Oh, Elsie." Andrew sighed. "I'm so sorry. But it could have been worse, though. Think on that," he added, trying to comfort her. "He could have been hanged."

"I know, but I'll never, ever see him again," cried Elsie. "He's as good as dead to me."

"Don't say that." Andrew's voice was gentle. "It's only for five years – not for life."

"Yes, but you know he'll never come back. He'll be set free and then he'll have to find some way to survive in Australia.

He'll never make enough money to come back to England." A fresh burst of tears poured down Elsie's cheeks. "And even if he did, I don't think he would want to," she whispered.

Andrew's face was filled with sorrow. "I'm so sorry, Elsie," he said. "This must be very hard for you."

"As hard as it is for me, it's worse for Mama." Elsie wiped at her tears. "I don't know what to do about her, Andrew. She can't take care of herself. I give her all of my wages, but it's just never enough. She never has enough to eat, and she always has to scrape and struggle to pay the rent. She's taken up some mending, but her hands are so weak and shaky that it takes her ages to do any sewing, and even then, it's often not very good." She sniffed, worry threatening to strangle her. "I'm so worried about her. What if she gets sick?" The fear overwhelmed her, and she covered her face with her hands. "She's already sick. And there's nobody, nobody to care for her, not now that Philip is gone."

"Hush, now." Andrew laid his other hand on Elsie's free shoulder, squeezing them both. "Please don't cry, Elsie. Calm yourself. It's going to be all right."

Elsie took a deep, shuddering breath and lowered her hands. She sniffed and wiped away her tears. "I don't know what to do," she whispered. She stared into his green eyes, and her heart was aching. "I think I'm going to have to find another job."

"Another job?" Andrew stepped back, his hands falling to his sides, his eyes widening. "Why?"

"I can't care for my mama now, not with having to stay here every night," Elsie said sadly. "I can't leave her alone all the time – not now that Philip's... gone for good. I need a job that will let me go home every night."

"But what kind of job would let you do that?" asked Andrew gently.

Elsie hung her head. "I've seen girls coming out of the match factory every evening," she murmured.

"No. No, no, no." Andrew shook his head sharply. "You can't become a match girl, Elsie – don't even think it. Those girls die of a horrible disease called phossy jaw, and there's no way to prevent it if you work in the match factory."

Elsie thought of the dead-eyed girls she'd seen walking down the street, the gaping wounds she'd seen on their cheeks. She shuddered. "Perhaps not a match factory, then," she said. "But there will be something else. There *must* be something else. I can't leave Mama alone anymore." Her eyes filled with tears again. "I'm sorry, Andrew, but I simply can't."

Andrew looked away, and Elsie saw real pain in his eyes. "I understand," he said, his voice thick. Then he turned on his heel and walked out, leaving Elsie alone with Mrs. Whiston's lukewarm tea and a terrible agony throbbing in her heart.

Elsie could hear Mama's coughing even before she entered the tenement building. She walked faster as she headed down the passage, hearing her heart pounding in her ears. Mama's coughs sounded wet and harsh, as if they were being ripped, red and raw, from deep inside her chest.

"Mama?" Elsie nudged the door open. "Mama, are you all right?"

One glance told her that Mama was far from all right. Instead of bustling around, Mama was huddled underneath a threadbare blanket on her sleeping mat. The same dress from Tuesday lay crumpled on the mat beside her, but the needle and thread were lying on top of it, untouched. She looked up with swimming eyes as Elsie came in, and her face was ashen.

"Oh, Mama." Elsie rushed to her side. "What is the matter? Are you ill?"

Mama gave another agonized cough before answering. "No, no, child, don't worry. I'm quite all right, I assure you."

"You don't sound very well," said Elsie. She felt Mama's forehead, relieved that it wasn't too hot to the touch. "What's wrong?"

"Just a bit of a chill, my dear," said Mama. "Don't worry." She tried to smile. "You didn't happen to bring something to eat...?"

"Of course, Mama. I found a grocer that was still open and bought you enough for the week." *I hope,* Elsie added silently, glancing up at the basket that she'd put down on the floor beside her. It looked pathetically small to contain sustenance for an entire week.

"Thank you, darling," said Mama. She struggled to sit up straighter, pushing the blanket aside. "I'll get something going for us, and—" With a slight whimper, she crumpled back to the floor, her face blanching even more.

"No. Sit right there, Mama." Elsie pushed her gently back down, realizing that her hands were shaking. "I'll make some supper for you. Don't worry."

As she put together some cold meat and bread, Elsie couldn't stop glancing over at Mama. She was leaning against the wall now, panting slightly; it was as if even the tiny effort of rising from her sleeping mat had drained her of all energy, and it scared Elsie. Would Mama still be here when she got back next Sunday? Or would she come home to find the tenement empty, stripped of even Mama's meager belongings, her body carted off sometime to a place that Elsie would never find -

No. Elsie shook her head firmly, her shaking hands gripping Mama's plate. She couldn't let that happen. She *wouldn't* let that happen. Walking back to Mama's sleeping mat, she knelt and held out the plate. "Here you go, Mama. There's some cheese, too. I know how you love cheese."

"Thanks, my love." Mama shakily took the plate and took a

hungry bite of the cold ham. Her eyes closed blissfully as she ate, and Elsie fancied that she could already see some color returning to Mama's cheeks.

"Feeling better?" she asked softly when Mama was done eating.

"Much." Mama smiled, handing Elsie her plate. She pulled her blanket up a little higher on her shoulders. "I'm sorry, my dear, I'm not very talkative today. I think I just need a little sleep."

"That's a good idea," said Elsie softly. She reached out, brushing some of her mother's graying hair behind her ear. "I'm going to leave my job," she said.

"What?" Mama's eyes snapped wide. She struggled upright again. "What are you talking about, Elsie?"

"I can't leave you here alone, Mama," said Elsie. She swallowed. "Who knows when Philip... um... when Philip's court case will be decided? I can't leave you by yourself. You need someone to care for you."

"Elsie, you can't leave your job," said Mama. "How will we survive?"

"I'll make a plan," said Elsie. "I'll figure something out – you know I will. But hush for now." She pulled the blanket back up, tucking it around Mama's shoulders. "Hush and rest a little. You're tired, Mama. Just rest."

She could tell by the look in Mama's eyes that she would have argued further if she'd had the strength. Instead, she just let out a fluttering sigh and sank back beneath the blankets. Elsie watched her, feeling sorrow swamp her. Watching her mother's exhausted face relax into sleep, she knew that she had no choice but to resign from Whiston Manor.

And she also knew that that would mean she would never see Andrew again.

CHAPTER 14

"I'm going to miss you," Elsie whispered, walking through the empty cottage, which had become her favorite refuge. She reached out, allowing her fingertips to brush the dusty kitchen wall as she headed toward the front door. "I had many, many happy dreams in here."

She sighed, standing on the threshold, and looked back longingly into the cozy little kitchen. "I wish it could have happened someday that I married Andrew and came to live here... but I suppose this is goodbye." Swallowing a lump in her throat, she took one last look and then stepped forward into the orchard.

There was a curious little chirp, and the robin alighted on a branch near Elsie. She knew the chances that this was the same robin were slim, but she liked to think it was. She didn't look at the bird, feeling tears prickle at her throat and behind her eyes.

"Yes, goodbye to you, too, little robin," she whispered. "Thank you for being my only friend." Looking up, she spotted an elegant figure through the parlor window, and her heart sank even further. "Well, almost my only friend. I wish he wasn't here today."

It was half past one, and Elsie knew that there was no delaying it any longer. Her lunchtime was past, and she would have to go up to Mrs. Whiston's room and resign – there was no way around it. Steeling herself, she headed back into the house.

Florence already had Mrs. Whiston's afternoon tea ready for her on the tray when Elsie walked into the kitchen. "Thank you, Florence," said Elsie, grabbing the tray.

"My pleasure, child." Florence gave her a searching look. "Are you all right?"

"Yes, thank you. I'm quite well," said Elsie, choking down the lump in her throat. She carried the tea up to the parlor to find that Andrew had arrived during her lunch time, just as she'd feared when she'd seen his silhouette through the window. He must have helped Mrs. Whiston out of bed after her usual nap. She sat in her armchair already, her mottled face looking grumpy and out of sorts with sleep.

"There you are," Mrs. Whiston spluttered as Elsie stepped

into the parlor. "I wondered when, if ever, you would realize that you're being paid to work – not to fool around outside all day."

"I apologize, Mrs. Whiston," said Elsie smoothly. She didn't look up at Andrew as she set the tray down on the table beside Mrs. Whiston's chair.

Mrs. Whiston glared at her. "I should hope you do," she snapped. "Now poke the fire at once. I'll catch my death in this ghastly temperature. I don't know what you mean by bringing me into this room, Andrew. Surely there are quicker ways to kill me if you really are out for my blood."

"Now, now, Grandmother." Andrew's tone was flatter than usual, and Elsie could feel him watching her as she bent to poke the fire. "I'm sure your fussing is not necessary."

"Do hurry up with that, girl," snapped Mrs. Whiston. "My tea is not going to serve itself, you know."

Elsie bit her tongue. She wanted to straighten up and tell Mrs. Whiston that she could serve her own tea – that she could do very much for herself, if she wasn't so fat and didn't like pretending to be a victim of everyone and everything. Instead, she turned around, folded her hands demurely in front of her, and said, "Mrs. Whiston, I'm terribly sorry, but I must give you my resignation."

There was a moment of perfect silence. Elsie could feel the shock rippling through the room like something physical.

It was Andrew who spoke. "What?"

Elsie still kept her eyes on Mrs. Whiston. "I have been honored to be of service to you," she said, "but I can no longer stay. I'm sorry."

Mrs. Whiston's eyes were popping. She simply stared at Elsie for a long few moments before speaking. "I don't accept your resignation."

It was Elsie's turn to be taken aback. "What?"

"No. You can't leave," said Mrs. Whiston. "At my age, I need a constant companion. I need someone who knows how to care for me – and you have finally become capable of that task. What do you think I would do if I had to train a new girl from the beginning, hmm? You almost killed me in your first few weeks. What do you think would happen to me?" Her eyes glittered menacingly. "You don't care for me—nobody does—but even you must have some kind of heart. You must care a little for a helpless old woman who needs your help."

"I'm sorry, Mrs. Whiston," said Elsie, trying to gather her scattered thoughts. "I understand, but there's no way that I can keep working here. My mother is sick, and I need to be home with her every night." She took a step toward the door. "I must resign. There is no other way."

"You selfish child," Mrs. Whiston snapped. "How can you do this to me? How could you be so heartless?"

Elsie wanted to run. To bolt down the hallway and never look back. She wanted to leave behind this miserable old woman and all of her abuse forever. She took another step toward the door, and only when she was at the threshold did she look over into Andrew's eyes. She had to see him just one last time, and the moment she looked at his face, she wished she hadn't.

The warmth and joy were simply gone from his expression; instead, there was a terrible, aching sorrow, a hollowness that echoed what Elsie was feeling in her own heart. She was gripped by an urge to run to him, to run into his arms and cling to him, breathing his scent and feeling his heart beating against her. She wanted to be near him, to be safe with him. Caught between wanting to flee and wanting to stay near him, she hovered in the doorway, hating the agony in his eyes.

"If you stay, I'll give you a bit more salary," said Mrs. Whiston. "And the cottage."

Both Andrew and Elsie whipped around to stare at her. "Excuse m-me, ma'am?" Elsie stammered.

"The cottage. You know – that tumbledown little thing in the orchard." Mrs. Whiston's tone was clipped and severe. "Did you think I wasn't aware of you snooping around in there like you had a right? I know everything, girl. If you stay on until I die, I will leave the cottage to you in my will and testament."

"You will?" said Andrew, staring.

Mrs. Whiston glared at him. "How well do you know me, Andrew?" she said. "I like to be modest, and I am a good and

A DAUGHTER'S DESPERATION

generous soul. I will help this young ragamuffin improve herself." She nodded at Elsie. "I need you to take care of me, and no one else. You're not much good, but everyone else I have had has been frankly abysmal. Stay on and you'll get a small raise and the cottage." She sniffed. "I can understand that kindness is quite beyond you, but perhaps you would stay if you were motivated by material gain."

Elsie realized that her jaw was hanging open. Looking over at Andrew, she saw that he, too, looked completely shocked. For a moment, she pictured herself and Andrew sitting at the kitchen table in the cottage with her red checkered curtains. She imagined them walking up the staircase hand in hand. Kissing their children goodnight in their bedrooms. Sitting on a warm sofa in front of the blazing fire together...

"Well?" Mrs. Whiston demanded. "What do you say? Are you staying?"

Elsie took a deep breath and pushed aside her fantasies with Andrew. She knew that if she could just cling on until Mrs. Whiston passed away, she could move herself and her mother into the cottage. They would never, ever have to pay rent again – they would have a safe place to stay, and half the battle would be won. And with a small raise, she could buy a bit more food for her mother. She knew that it was worth struggling on for now.

"Yes," she whispered. "Yes, I'm staying."

"Good," said Mrs. Whiston. "Now, go to the kitchen and

bring me something to eat at once. Can't you see that I'm starving? I'll die of malnutrition sooner rather than later if you stay so careless, you miserable girl."

"Y-yes, ma'am." Elsie scurried away.

She had not yet reached the kitchen when she heard the footsteps behind her.

"Elsie! Elsie, wait."

Elsie turned. Andrew was hurrying after her, and he was wide-eyed, a smile playing over his face. "I can't believe it!" he gasped. "I can't believe what my grandmother just did." He laughed, spreading his arms. "Isn't it incredible?"

"It's wonderful," Elsie said. She was trembling with excitement. "Why do you think she did it?"

"It seems my grandmother does have a soft spot – and it's you," Andrew laughed.

Elsie shook her head. "On the contrary, I think you're the soft spot," she said. She realized that she was grinning. "I can't wait to tell my mama."

Then she sobered. "Do you think she's telling the truth? I mean, can it be true? She'll really give me the *cottage*?"

"Grandmother has many faults, as you're well aware. But I've never known her to lie."

Elsie began to smile again. She couldn't believe her fortune. Simply, couldn't believe it.

"Oh, Elsie, I'm so glad," Andrew said.

The next moment, to Elsie's surprise, Andrew's arms were around her. It was only for a second, but he squeezed her fervently, pulling her close to his chest. "I'm so glad for you," he whispered, his warm breath brushing against her ear, making goosebumps erupt all over her body. "You deserve it."

The embrace was over as quickly as it had come, and then Andrew was hurrying back up the hallway, leaving Elsie alone at the kitchen door. She felt as though she had just been filled with sunshine, her entire being overflowing with golden light.

A grin spread over her face. From this moment onward, things could only possibly get better.

CHAPTER 15

Elsie had been waiting all week for this moment, but she still felt a pang of worry as she hurried through the streets toward the tenement building. It was nothing but the excitement and elation over the cottage that had borne Elsie through the past week of worrying over her mother. Now, she jogged down the street, her feet splashing in the watery mud, trying her best to avoid the worst of the puddles.

"Mama!" she shouted as she reached the front door of the tenement. "Mama, I'm home."

There was no response, and Elsie's heart felt as though it had stopped dead inside her chest. Why was there no response? Had Mama not heard her? "Are you here? Mama? Mama!"

She all but kicked the door open and relief flooded her veins. Mama was sitting by the rickety table, painstakingly filling the little pot with warm water. A headscarf was bound tightly around her head and ears, but there was more color in her face than last time.

"Oh, hello, dear," she said, putting down the jug and unwrapping her headscarf.

"Mama, you scared me." Elsie sighed in relief, setting down her shopping basket on the table. She leaned over and kissed her mother's cheek.

"Sorry, dear. I'm just getting over that nasty head cold from last week, and I decided to keep my scarf on so that the chill doesn't get into my ears." Mama smiled.

Elsie knew that Mama had suffered with much worse than a mere head cold, but she was glad to see that she looked so much better.

"That's all right," she said. "Look – I've brought you some vegetables. Can I make you some soup?"

"That would be lovely. Thank you," said Mama. "Here, let me help."

Elsie almost danced with impatience as Mama started to peel and chop the potatoes that Elsie had brought. She took some green beans out of the shopping basket and broke off the ends, tossing the beans whole into the pot of water that she had put into the fireplace. All week, Elsie had been waiting to tell Mama the glad news, but now that she was actually here, she found herself suddenly tongue-tied somehow.

"There," said Mama at length, scraping the potatoes from a tin plate into the pot. "All done. Now, sit here with me and tell me all about your week." She sat by the kitchen table, and Elsie joined her. Mama smiled. "Your eyes are sparkling like you want to tell me something good."

"Actually, Mama, I do have something to tell you." Elsie took a deep breath. "Mrs. Whiston told me that she will leave her cottage to me in her will when she dies."

Mama's face froze. She stared at Elsie for a moment. "That can't be true. Did you hear her right? Do you think she meant it?"

"I know she did. She had a solicitor come in during the week and change her will for her," said Elsie happily. "She's serious, Mama. As soon as she passes away, that cottage will be ours."

"Elsie." Mama reached over and grabbed Elsie's hands in hers, tears of joy running down her cheeks. "Oh, Elsie, I'm so glad for you. You deserve it over and over." She laughed, sniffing. "I can't believe it. This is the most amazing news. I've never heard the like."

"I know." Elsie grinned. "We're going to live there someday, Mama. You and me will be safely tucked up in there, and we'll never have to pay rent again. It'll be warm and beautiful, and I just know we're going to be so happy there."

"Yes. Yes, we are." Mama laughed. "You and Philip and I, all safely together again."

A DAUGHTER'S DESPERATION

The mention of Philip's name made Elsie's heart sink. She looked down, pulling her hands away from Mama's, and realized that it was now or never. "Mama," she said, softly, "about Philip. There's something I must tell you."

She looked up, and as quickly as the elation had come to Mama's face, it was gone again. "What is it?" Mama whispered.

"Philip's... Philip's gone, Mama," Elsie whispered. "They sentenced him to five years in Australia." Hot tears filled her eyes. "I'm so sorry. He's gone."

A silence filled the little room, a silence so heavy that it seemed ready to stifle everything, to strangle the very air that Elsie was trying to breathe through her hot, choked throat. Then, Mama's trembling hands found hers again.

"It will be all right, my girl," Mama whispered. "I expected it. I just..." She paused, and her voice was shaking. "I can't bear to lose your brother, too," she whispered.

Elsie looked up to see a tear rolling down Mama's cheek. "You won't, Mama," she said. "I know you won't. In five years, he'll be back. You'll see. He'll come back."

Mama nodded, biting her lip, the tears spilling freely down her cheeks now. "Yes," she whispered. "Five years. Just five years."

Fear gripped Elsie. She squeezed her mother's fingers, aware that her heart was pounding. *Please, Mama,* she thought. *Please just live another five years.*

"Do you mean to kill me, girl?" Mrs. Whiston moaned. "Look at all the coal dust that you've made. You're destroying my home. You're polluting my lungs. Oh, have you no compassion?"

"No, ma'am. Sorry, ma'am." Elsie grimaced, using the fire tongs to carefully place another coal into the hearth. If she'd thought that Mrs. Whiston would treat her better now that she'd added Elsie to her will, she'd been sorely mistaken. If anything, the old lady was crankier than ever.

"Why don't you add more coal to the fire?" Mrs. Whiston demanded as Elsie put down the tongs. "Honestly, girl, this isn't some pauper's hovel. Do you know much coal it takes to heat a grand house like this? You'll let me catch my death, I swear you will. I have a very delicate constitution, you know. The tiniest fluctuations in temperature may affect me terribly." She drew her shawl more tightly around herself with a disdainful little sniff. "As you should know by now."

"Of course. Sorry, ma'am." Elsie added some more coal and had just grabbed a poker to stir the fire up a bit when a sonorous tone echoed through the house. It was only the doorbell, but to Elsie it always sounded like the pealing of a church bell. She shot to her feet, excitement thumping in her heart.

"Who can that be?" muttered Mrs. Whiston, fussing with her shawl. "What dreadful timing they have, with the butler off sick today. Oh, I wish they would just go away."

There was only one person who would arrive unannounced at Whiston Manor, and Elsie knew exactly who it had to be. She'd never had the chance to open the door for him before, as the butler always attended to such things.

"I'll get the door, ma'am," she said, trying to hide her excitement.

Mrs. Whiston sighed. "I suppose you'd better," she said. "Hurry up, now. It won't do for you to leave me unattended."

Elsie tried not to run as she headed out of the parlor. It had been a long and lonely week at the manor – and she'd been praying for days that her only real friend might turn up for a surprise visit, as he sometimes did.

It seemed to take an age to reach the door. When she finally did, she knew that she was smiling. "Andrew!" she cried, pulling the great doors wide. "How are—"

Her glad words died on her lips. Elsie stared, her heart sinking, at what looked like her worse nightmare: *two* Mrs. Whiston's. She blinked to make sure she wasn't seeing double. The two women standing in front of her were such close copies of Mrs.

Whiston and of each other that the scene felt like a surreal bad dream. They glared down at her with identical expressions of disgust, their chins wobbling in disapproval as they inspected her over their spectacles. Their curvaceous girths were nothing short of magnificent, and their paunchy cheeks were the exact echo of Mrs. Whiston's, minus most of the wrinkles. The only difference between them and Elsie's mistress was their age.

"Who are you?" Elsie blurted before she realized what she was doing.

"The proper question," said the woman on the left, "is who are *you*?"

"Agatha," said the woman on the right, "I do believe it must be – you know – *her*."

The two women exchanged glances, then leaned over to stare at Elsie, coming so close to her that Elsie could smell their sickly-sweet perfume. Their eyes were as sharp and cold as Mrs. Whiston's, and something about them made Elsie tremble in her shoes.

"I do believe you're right, Sophronia," said Agatha after a long contemplation. "Yet, could it be that Granny would allow such a dreadfully scruffy-looking little thing to come anywhere near her?"

"You know that Granny's not well," said Sophronia. "She's probably hallucinating."

They gave each other a conspiratorial look.

"You must be right," said Agatha. "She must be quite out of her mind."

"In that case," said Sophronia, "we will simply have to change it."

"Now, now, don't get ahead of yourself, my dear," said Agatha. "We must first find out that it is true."

"Yes, yes. We must," agreed Sophronia.

Elsie was starting to feel rather forgotten. "Excuse me?" she said politely. "May I help you, ma'ams?"

"Indeed, you can," the women chorused with disconcerting synchronization. They stared at her, their focus sharp.

"Take us to Granny," said Agatha. "Why would you leave us standing out here like two strangers? Why, the very thought of it!"

"Yes, take us to Granny at once," said Sophronia.

"'Granny...?" asked Elsie, knowing of course precisely who they meant,

"Your mistress," retorted Agatha.

"Mrs. Whiston," said Sophronia.

"Of course." Elsie's stomach clenched. She'd had no idea that Mrs. Whiston had other relatives in the area. "Right away, ma'am. This way."

Walking up to the parlor, the women were frighteningly silent, walking side by side directly behind Elsie, their eyes unblinking every time that she glanced back toward them. They made her skin crawl, and the whole time, she wondered why they had come to the manor. One thing was for sure – it wasn't simply a social visit. Elsie couldn't shake the horrible suspicion that the cottage had something to do with it, but then, maybe she was just being unnecessarily concerned.

"Ma'am," Elsie called, knocking on the parlor door. "Your granddaughters are here to see you."

She pushed the door wide, and Mrs. Whiston glared up from her chair, her mouth twisting bitterly.

"Well, well, well," she said. "I must be even more ill than even I thought I was, if you two vultures have come to see me."

The sisters stepped inside and gave simpering smiles. "Now, don't be like that, Granny," said Agatha.

"Why else would you be here?" Mrs. Whiston gave them a suspicious glare. "All interest you have in me has to do with what you'll inherit. Apart from that, neither of you have had any time for me since your parents died."

"You know that's not true, Granny," said Sophronia.

"I know it is," Mrs. Whiston returned, "but I suppose you'd better gave a seat." She gestured at the settee. "I'll send my dreadful little maid for some tea."

"Actually, Granny," said Agatha, "we would like her to stay here in the room." She shot Elsie a smug glance.

Sophronia did the same. "Yes, we would," she said. "You see, we've got something to discuss with you – and *her*." She spat the word as if it were made of acid.

Elsie's stomach twisted with fear. She froze by the door, her hands shaking.

"Ah. I suppose I should have known that you would come." Mrs. Whiston interlaced her hands and laid them on her tremendous belly.

"We're just concerned for you, Granny," simpered Agatha. "You see, we heard from a friend of a friend—"

"—of my husband," Sophronia chipped in.

"Yes, a friend of a friend of my husband," Agatha continued, "who works at a legal firm, that you had your solicitor make some... ah... *changes* to your will."

"Indeed, I did," said Mrs. Whiston. "Although what it's got to do with you two harpies, I wouldn't possibly know."

"It's not about what it's got to do with *us*," said Agatha. "It's about your... how can I put it..."

"Frame of mind," suggested Sophronia.

"Yes, your frame of mind," said Agatha.

Mrs. Whiston narrowed her eyes. "My frame of mind is

perfectly intact, I can assure you," she snapped. "And either way, it has precious little to do with you two." She glared over at Elsie. "You, girl. Don't you remember that you were poking the fire before this rude intrusion? Get it done."

"Yes, ma'am," Elsie said. She hurried over to the fire, aware that both the sisters were glaring at her.

"Then we can only think that your solicitor must have made a mistake, Granny," said Agatha.

"Yes, he must have," Sophronia concurred.

"Why on earth would you think that?" snapped Mrs. Whiston. "I understand that he is an incompetent imbecile, but I've spent my life surrounded by such people. I know how to manipulate them. My will is exactly as I want it, despite his best efforts."

"I don't think it possibly can be, Granny," said Agatha. "Because if it is, then it means you've left that precious little cottage in the woods to... to..."

Sophronia raised a sausage-like finger and pointed it accusingly at Elsie. "To *her*," she crowed.

There was a long moment of silence. Elsie wished she could crawl up the chimney and disappear.

"In that case," said Mrs. Whiston, slowly, "all is exactly as I want it to be." She fixed the two sisters with a challenging glare. "Your concerns have been addressed. You may leave now."

"But Granny, why would you do such a thing?" wailed Agatha.

"What's it to you?" snapped Mrs. Whiston. "You're already inheriting the entire manor house and all of its contents."

"Yes, but we're not getting the ships, Granny," moaned Sophronia.

"Nor the cottage," cried Agatha. "Why would you let the cottage, that beautiful little cottage, go to some simpering little street-rat like this?"

"How could you be so heartless, Granny?" said Sophronia, dramatically raising a hand to her brow.

Elsie would have giggled if they had been talking about anyone but her. Now she felt caught in the crossfire, staring from Mrs. Whiston to the granddaughters and back again as if some ghastly game were taking place in front of her, using her future as the ball.

"It's not me that's being heartless," said Mrs. Whiston, her tone clipped and dangerous. "It's the girl."

The two granddaughters stared at Elsie, their gazes pinning her to the spot.

"What has she done?" demanded Agatha, rising to her feet.

"I'll have her hide if she's hurt you, Granny." Sophronia followed suit.

"She's tried to resign," said Mrs. Whiston curtly. Shocked, the two granddaughters flopped back onto the settee and stared at her. "That simply won't do, you know," said Mrs. Whiston. "She knows how to care for me, even if she doesn't do a very good job. I don't have the strength to train a new maid at my age. She needs to stay." She shrugged. "And the cottage was the perfect way to make her do it."

"Oh, how *could* you, Granny?" Agatha was so dramatic that Elsie wouldn't have been surprised if she had started gnashing her teeth. "You've stolen from your own granddaughters. How could you have done it?"

"Easily," snapped Mrs. Whiston. "I just did. Now leave, both of you. You're upsetting my digestion."

The two sisters glared at Mrs. Whiston for a few more moments, their faces pale with rage. Then Agatha got to her feet. "Come on, Sophronia," she said icily. "*Clearly,* we're not welcome here."

"I'll show you out," stammered Elsie, straightening up from her place by the hearth.

"Thank you," said Sophronia sweetly, but the glitter in her eye was evil, and Elsie could feel herself shaking with fear as she led them down to the front door. And not without good reason. As she opened the doors for them, Agatha stopped and leaned in so that her wobbling chins were just inches from Elsie's face.

"You will never get that cottage," she hissed. "Mark my words."

And with that, they were both gone.

CHAPTER 16

Elsie stood in the cottage doorway, gazing into its dusty interior, her heart feeling as heavy as a lump of stone in her chest. She'd hoped that coming here was going to make her feel better, yet staring into the kitchen – the kitchen that would someday hopefully be hers – only made her miss Mama even more. She wished she could have the cottage now already, that she could already have fixed it and furnished it and brought Mama here—that Mama could be bustling around the way she had once when she'd been a housekeeper in a manor just like this one.

Elsie pictured the scene; a younger Mama, with rosy cheeks and a merry laugh, cooking and cleaning after work, smacking Philip's bottom when he tried to get into trouble, scooping Elsie up in her arms and dancing around the kitchen as she sang a lively hymn.

"Oh, Mama," Elsie whispered, squeezing her eyes shut against the tears that prickled behind them. "You've got to hold on. You've got to live long enough to live here with me."

"I thought I'd find you here."

Elsie turned, a smile spreading over her features as relief gushed through her body like sunshine. "Mr. Whiston!" she said. He'd given her permission to call him Andrew, but sometimes, still, she felt self-conscious about it. Once again, she wanted to run to him, to throw herself into his arms. But instead, all she could do was smile, hoping that her eyes were saying everything that her words were not allowed to.

Andrew was standing in the footpath, his hands buried deep in his pockets. He gave her his crooked smile, his head to one side. "Inspecting your new home?" he asked softly.

"It's not my home yet." Elsie sighed, reaching out to touch the nearest wall with loving fingertips. "In fact, I'm worried that it might never be."

"What do you mean?" Andrew raised his eyebrows. "The solicitor's changed the will – everything is done. Nothing can stop you from getting the cottage now."

Elsie sighed. "Unless someone manages to change your grandmother's mind."

Andrew's face fell. "Oh, no," he groaned. "Don't tell me that *they* were here."

"If by 'they' you mean your two older sisters, then yes, they were here." Elsie tried to laugh.

Andrew grimaced. "Charming, aren't they?"

Elsie paused. "Well, they certainly take after their grandmother."

"I'm sorry." Andrew laughed, coming over to her. He rested his hands on her shoulders again, and she felt a jolt of electricity run through her body as his green eyes gazed deeply into hers. "What did they say to you?" he murmured. "What happened?"

"They were... upset that your grandmother put me in her will." Elsie swallowed. "I had no idea you even had sisters, Andrew."

"I know. I try to forget that I have them," said Andrew wryly. "I can't believe that they'd cause trouble about this, though. They're inheriting the entire manor. What could they want with the cottage?"

"I don't know," said Elsie, "but they want to change your grandmother's mind."

Andrew shook his head. "I wouldn't worry about that if I were you. She's a stubborn old goat, as you know. It's not that easy to get her to change her mind about *anything*."

"You think so?" Elsie gazed up at him, her eyes begging him for hope.

"I know so. Don't worry." Andrew gave her shoulders a light squeeze. "Nothing's going to stop Grandmother from doing what she wants – and apparently what she wants is to give you the cottage."

"I hope so." Elsie sighed. "Do you think they'll come here again?"

"Oh, they will." Andrew gave her a sorry smile. "Unfortunately, they're just as stubborn. They'll try to weasel their way into her good books, you can be sure of that."

Elsie's shoulders slumped. "They're a bit scary, Andrew," she confessed. "It wasn't nice having them here."

"I know." Andrew was still gazing at her, his eyes deep with emotion. "Speaking of the inheritance, at least I know I'm in the will, too. I believe I'm supposed to get my grandfather's investment in ships going across to the New World. And once that happens, I'm going to make your life so much better."

His voice was rough with sincerity, and as Elsie gazed at him, she thought she had never seen anything brighter or deeper than his eyes. Her lips parted, and she was about to ask him what he meant when there was a shriek from the manor.

"Where is that girl?" Mrs. Whiston bellowed.

The spell broke. Elsie stepped back, Andrew's hands falling to his sides.

"Sounds like your grandmother needs me," Elsie stammered,

suddenly stumbling under the weight of the awkwardness that had filled the air.

"Elsie—" Andrew began. But Elsie was already running back to the manor house as fast as her legs would take her.

CHAPTER 17

Elsie's feet pounded on the cobblestones. Each step was a jolt that she felt through her aching legs, up her stiff back and through the very top of her head, but she had no choice. Clutching her bag close to her chest, she pushed herself to run faster, her breath rushing, her heart thundering. Behind her, she could hear them yipping and yelling, calling out ugly names and mocking cries. They were gaining on her, and Elsie knew it.

She swung onto the main road of the slum, if you could call it a road. Her feet slithered in mud, and she slipped, almost falling. For a heart-stopping moment, the dirt rushed up to meet her; then one foot found a stone for purchase, and she was running again. She risked a glance back and saw that they'd gained a few yards. They were close enough now that the dirty moonlight, sullied and diluted by factory smoke, illuminated their faces: pinched and pale, even younger than hers. But their lanky limbs were strong and masculine, and they drove them forward with a force and determination born of hunger.

She didn't want to think what they'd do if they caught her. So she didn't think. She just ran, putting everything into it, her arms locked around the bag as tightly as possible.

At last, an alleyway, off to her right. Elsie ducked down it, diving behind a pile of rubbish. There was a barrel here, its mouth gaping open, lying on its side. Dirty water pooled inside it, but Elsie had no choice. She dove into it and pulled a rag over the entrance, masking her hiding place. Her hands were wet and filthy when she pressed them over her nose and mouth, hoping to muffle her breathing.

Their footsteps were close now. Their voices even closer, shouting roughly. She heard them skid to a halt just outside the barrel, their feet splashing in dirt and water.

"Where'd she go?" cried one voice breathlessly. The sound was that of a child, but the emotion behind it had an ageless harshness.

"There!" another shouted. "That way! Down the alley!"

Elsie cringed, motionless, holding her breath as well as she could, until she was sure that they were all gone. Then, exhausted, she crawled out of the barrel. Her feet were sore and bleeding from running, but it wasn't much farther now.

Gathering her bag tighter in her arms, Elsie limped toward the tenement.

When she got there, Mama was still asleep. Elsie tiptoed inside as quietly as she could, setting the bag down on the little table. Opening it softly, she took out a few lumps of coal. Two were a little damp from huddling in the barrel, but there were three others that were still serviceable. She laid them in the hearth and grabbed a box of matches from the mantelpiece. When she shook the box, she heard the lonely rattle of a single match.

"Elsie?" Mama's sleepy voice came from the mat. Elsie turned, hurrying over to her. "Mama," she whispered, crouching beside her. She touched her mother's arm; her skin was icy to the touch. "Why did you let the fire go out? You'll catch your death like this."

"Sorry, darling." Mama cleared her throat, swallowing painfully. "Why are you here? You came last night, as well. Won't you get into trouble?"

"Mrs. Whiston almost always sleeps from one to four in the morning, Mama," said Elsie. "That gives me just enough time to slip out and check on you."

"It's dangerous out there this time of night."

Elsie knew that only two well. Being chased through the streets like that—well, this wasn't the first time. But it was a danger she had to face if she wanted to continue caring for her mother.

Mama studied her shrewdly, even though her movements were weak and sluggish as she pulled the blankets closer around her shoulders. "And when do you sleep?" she whispered.

Elsie didn't answer. She turned back to the fire, took the single match out of the box, and whispered a little prayer before striking it. It flared up, and Elsie hurried to light the coal. To her relief, it began to smolder.

"There you are," she said. "It'll warm the room right up."

Mama was still watching her sharply. "Where did you buy coal at this time of night, Elsie?"

Elsie thought of the coal-scuttle standing by the fireplace in the parlor, always brimming full, and tried to push aside the wave of guilt that hung over her.

"Don't mind that now, Mama," she said, going back over to her mother and tucking her back into bed. "Hush now. Just sleep – I'll put some soup on for you to eat in the morning."

Mama settled back onto the mat, and Elsie smoothed her hair out of her face. The older woman's eyes were concerned, but already growing heavy again. "Elsie," she murmured as she closed her eyes.

"Yes, Mama?"

"I love you, my darling."

Elsie fought against a lump in her throat. She stared at the flickering flames that had started to lick around the edges of the coals, feeling suddenly utterly alone.

"I love you too, Mama," she whispered.

※

WHEN ELSIE HAD SLIPPED BACK INTO THE MANOR AROUND three o' clock that morning, Mrs. Whiston had been awake. Elsie had had to run as fast as she could up all the flights of stairs to reach her room. That left Mrs. Whiston with one of her covers slipping off of her for an entire five minutes – a state of affairs that, even after some more sleep and her usual breakfast, still left her cranky.

Elsie could barely bring herself to care. Now, at mid-morning, she felt half asleep where she stood by the bookshelf in Mrs. Whiston's library, reading out loud from the row of titles on the shelf. Her tongue felt fat and furry with exhaustion as it struggled to form around the words.

"What about *The Pickwick Papers?*" she read from the spine of the nearest book.

"Oh, I'm quite sick of Mr. Dickens," said Mrs. Whiston grumpily. "He so insists on pandering to the common and useless ideals of the *working class*." She pronounced the last two words with such vehemence that Elsie could almost hear the venom dripping from them.

"All right, ma'am," she said. "How about *Vanity Fair?*"

"Too new," sniffed Mrs. Whiston. "I won't read new fiction, you know – it's tasteless to a palate as distinguished and educated as my own."

"*Ivanhoe?*"

"Oh, much too old and dry. Honestly, girl, one can see that you have no education beyond what's necessary to read the titles of those books."

Elsie didn't bother to disagree, mainly because what Mrs. Whiston said was true. "Yes, ma'am. *Wuther... Wuthering um...?*"

"*Wuthering Heights?* Women have no place writing books," spat Mrs. Whiston. "I don't know why that book is even in my library. Written by an insolent young upstart, no doubt – although I can see why *you* would be attracted to it. Its author clearly doesn't know her place, an ailment from which you also seem to suffer."

Elsie gritted her teeth. "How about *The I-Idylls of the King?*"

"Oh, never mind." Mrs. Whiston rolled her eyes dramatically. "Honestly, I don't know if you even have a brain at all, girl. You know how I despise poetry. I don't know why I even keep you on. You seem incapable of serious thought – or even memory."

Elsie didn't have the strength to deal with Mrs. Whiston today like she normally did. She gulped hard at the lump in her throat and turned to the old lady, desperate. Perhaps she could try appealing to Mrs. Whiston's better nature – if she possessed such a thing. "I'm very distracted today," she began.

"Clearly," sniffed Mrs. Whiston, giving her a disdainful glare.

"It's my mother, ma'am," said Elsie. "She's ill. She's truly, terribly—"

"A common state for poor people." Mrs. Whiston shook her head. "Why you all have to insist on being ill all the time, nobody knows. No contribution to society at all."

Elsie hung her head. "She's all alone. She needs me."

Mrs. Whiston's eyes hardened. "Are you trying to resign again?"

"No, ma'am. I was just wondering…" Elsie took a deep breath, gathering her courage. "I was wondering if I could bring her to the manor. There's so much room in the servants' quarters. Just for a few nights. Just until—"

"Absolutely not." Mrs. Whiston's voice had the finality of a prison door slamming shut. "Does this look like the workhouse to you? The government insists on putting up churches and workhouses and what-have-you for all the poor and sick that seem to be lying around everywhere – let her go to one of those."

Elsie felt sick at the idea of her frail, gentle mother in the brutal workhouse. She opened her mouth…

"Not one more word." Mrs. Whiston jabbed her walking stick threateningly in Elsie's direction. "Not one."

"Leave me," Mrs. Whiston's said harshly. Feeling tears burst down her cheeks, Elsie backed away. "Go," Mrs. Whiston bellowed. "Only come back when you're ready to behave according to your station."

Elsie stumbled toward the door. She pushed the door open and half fell into the hallway, almost crashing directly into two ponderous forms that had appeared just outside the door. Dread filled Elsie's heart as she looked up into the twin glares of Agatha and Sophronia.

"Hello, girl," sneered Agatha.

"Nice to see you," purred Sophronia, with arsenic sweetness.

"Girls," crowed Mrs. Whiston from inside. "*Do* come in."

The twins' smirks widened. They gave Elsie a last, disdainful glance and then swept into the room.

PART III

CHAPTER 18

Three Years Later

A THIN TRICKLE OF SOUP DRIBBLED DOWN MRS. WHISTON'S chins, disappearing into the folds of her shriveled neck. Elsie shuddered a little, knowing that she'd be the one who'd have to try and clean it out of there again. She hid her disgust as well as she could and scraped up another spoonful of soup. "Come on," she said gently. "Just a little more."

Mrs. Whiston glared at her, shifting among the pillows that were holding her up. "I know I need a little more. What do you want me to do about the fact that I don't have the strength for more?"

"Just try," Elsie wheedled, raising the spoon. "It'll do you good, ma'am."

Mrs. Whiston let out an agonized groan, and Elsie felt real pity tugging at her heart. The old woman was feeble now, her limbs only capable of twitching sluggishly in protest, but her eyes still burned as bright and fierce as ever.

"Of course, it'll do me good," she snapped half-heartedly. "Do you think I'd hire a total idiot for a cook? Well, I hired one for a maid, but it's not your place to question that. Just give me that."

Elsie obediently spooned the soup into Mrs. Whiston's mouth, struggling to keep it going in the right direction. The old woman spluttered and sucked at it, snorting and fighting to get it down. When she had swallowed, she flopped back onto her pillows, panting with effort. Elsie mutely dipped a flannel in the basin of warm water beside the bed and gently cleaned Mrs. Whiston's face and neck.

"There you are, ma'am," she said soothingly. "You'll feel better now."

"I think I'm past ever feeling better," growled Mrs. Whiston. "Can't you see that I'm dying?"

Elsie sat still for a long moment, gazing down at the woman who had been a part of her days for so many years. The vast shape that had once made the bed groan with every toss and turn had been reduced now, to a skeleton wrapped in voluminous folds of loose and flabby skin. Her teeth were yellowed and rotting, protruding like a horse's; her eyes were buried deeply, not in paunchy cheeks, but in hollow sockets and ringed with dark shadows. Even Mrs. Whiston's hair was pale and stringy now, dangling and clutching desperately around her face as it struggled to hold on.

Yes, Elsie answered in her thoughts. *I can see that you're dying.*

Instead, she said, "You're just feeling a little low right now, ma'am." She dropped the flannel back into the basin and pulled the covers up tightly around Mrs. Whiston's bony shoulders. "You'll feel better after you've had a bit of a sleep."

"That's fiddlesticks, and you know it," Mrs. Whiston commented. "I'm not going to last very long. You know it and I know it – and those dreadful grandchildren of mine know it just as well. I can see them all circling like vultures over my carcass. All they want to do is pick apart all the beautiful things I've ever had."

"Now, ma'am, that's not true," said Elsie, plumping up the pillows. "I know that your grandson cares very deeply for you."

Mrs. Whiston glared at her narrowly. "I notice that you conveniently avoid mentioning yourself," she snapped. "Never mind. I know that you don't care for me – I have known ever since I first hired you." She relented slightly. "Although I know that Andrew's a good boy. But those granddaughters of mine – argh! They're terrible, honestly. I don't know what I've done to deserve such ungrateful souls in my life."

"Couldn't say, ma'am," said Elsie diplomatically.

"You're as bad as the rest of them," snapped Mrs. Whiston.

Elsie straightened up. "Can I bring you anything more?"

Mrs. Whiston stared at her for a long, long moment. Her eyes burned, but her hand reached out to Elsie, the fingers fluttering. Without thinking, Elsie grabbed it. The old lady's grip was as fervent as it was feeble, and she stared into Elsie's eyes for a moment that seemed to last for an eternity. She said nothing, but the expression in her eyes was unreadable. Elsie couldn't tell if it was anger, sorrow, fear, hope or a mixture of all four.

Abruptly, Mrs. Whiston let go. Her hand flopped back onto the bed. "No," she said shortly. "That'll be all for now. Thank you."

It was Elsie's turn to stare. In all the hours, and for all the thousands of tiny tasks she'd performed for the old lady, she had never once heard those words of gratitude from her mouth. "Ma'am?"

"Go," snapped Mrs. Whiston. "I need some sleep."

Elsie slipped out of the room as quietly as she could, taking the basin and flannel with her. She was on her way to the nearest lavatory to dump the dirty water when she heard familiar footsteps just down the hall. A smile flooded her heart and features, and she quickened her step. "Hello?" she called out, hopefully.

"Hello!" Andrew popped into sight from around the corner, a grin spread over his face. "Just the person that I was looking for."

Elsie laughed. She put the basin on her hip and paused, smiling, as Andrew came closer. "How are you today?" she asked. "It feels like forever since you were last here."

"Only two days," Andrew said. "Although, you're quite right. It does feel like forever." He reached out, his fingertips brushing her cheek for a moment, and Elsie felt her heart flip over. "Is Grandmother awake?"

"She's just gone to sleep," said Elsie. "She had a rough night – I was up and down every couple of hours checking on her."

"In that case, I'll let her rest." Andrew gracefully proffered an arm. "Would you care to walk with me while she reposes, fair lady?"

Elsie laughed and raised the basin slightly. "Only if my basin can come, too."

"I think perhaps we should dump that out first," said Andrew.

After making a brief detour to the lavatory, Elsie met Andrew at the front door. They headed into the garden together, and

Elsie easily slipped her arm through Andrew's, knowing that the other servants would all be on their lunch hour by now. They strolled together slowly, their feet crunching on the fresh snow that lay thickly on every surface.

Above them, the sky was a picturesque blue, so pure and cold that Elsie thought her steaming breath might just turn to diamonds where it touched the air. She allowed herself to lean a little closer to Andrew, allowing her hip and shoulder to bump against his warm body with every step.

"I wish we could be like this more often," Andrew murmured.

"Like what?" asked Elsie.

"You know. You and I, walking together – as if..." Andrew trailed off, but Elsie knew what he meant. As if she could really have been an eligible young lady for him to court. As if they really were a young couple like all the other young couples whose lives she envied so much.

"We have this moment, at least," Elsie said, squeezing his arm. Andrew looked down at her, his smile a little sad. "Yes," he said gently. "Yes, we do."

They walked a little further, venturing underneath the bending boughs of the orchard, each heavily laden with a burden of fresh snow. Elsie spotted the tracks of a fox disappearing into the trees and wished that she and Andrew could both follow them to whatever safe place the wild things could go.

"How is your mother?" Andrew asked at length.

"She's..." Elsie paused, sighing. "She's done better than I thought she would. Honestly, Andrew, I don't know how she made it through last winter. Every time I see her, she's a little weaker." She swallowed. "A little less able to care for herself. And now that your grandmother is weaker too, I can never get away to care for her."

"At least Grandmother is paying you a little better now."

"Yes. I can't complain," said Elsie. "That's probably the only reason why Mama is still alive. I've been able to feed her more. And once, we even had a doctor in. I'm grateful."

Andrew smiled at her and then sobered. "Is Grandmother still getting weaker, too?"

"Yes, she is," said Elsie sadly. "She hardly eats now, Andrew, and I know that she's in a lot of pain."

Andrew cocked his head, staring at her curiously. "It sounds like you feel sorry for her."

"I do," said Elsie. "It must be terrible to be in so much pain."

"But why would you feel anything for my grandmother? All she's ever done is to make your life miserable."

Elsie considered the question for a moment. She could glimpse the cottage between the trees now, its empty black windows looking like closed eyes.

"I've cared for your grandmother for five years, Andrew," she said. "I've always tried my best to be as good and kind and gentle as I possibly could for her, and she's grown on me a little over the years." She laughed. "At least now that she's a frail old lady, she's not as scary as she used to be. She almost managed to whack me with her walking stick a few times when she was still quicker."

Andrew shook his head. "You truly are a wonderful person, Elsie. Do you know that?"

Elsie felt her face heating. She looked away. "Not as wonderful as you," she whispered.

They paused, now in the doorway of the cottage. Snow had blown in over its floor, but its walls still stood as strong as they had when Elsie had wandered and daydreamed in its rooms when she was younger. Now she stared up at Andrew and saw that he had become a man; his shoulders were broad and strong, his jaw smoothly shaven.

"I'll miss the daft old bat," he murmured, gazing into her eyes. "But I can't wait for you and your mama to come and live in this cottage."

"That's if your sisters didn't manage to take it," Elsie answered softly.

"They haven't. Not yet," said Andrew. He reached up, brushing a stray strand of Elsie's dark hair out of her face. "Just hold on a little longer, Elsie. You're going to be safe, either way. You and your mother are going to be safe and warm. I'll make sure of it."

Elsie gazed at him, feeling her whole heart flood into her eyes. She wanted to reach up, cup his perfect face in her shaking hands, and press her lips to his. But she didn't know who might be watching, so she settled for leaning forward instead, resting her head against his shoulder. Andrew let his chin rest on the top of her head, his arms loosely around her. She knew that even being seen standing like this would start the gossip mills turning, but it felt so wonderful to be standing there like that.

Over the years, she and Andrew had drawn closer and closer together. She loved him. She knew that without a doubt. She didn't know how he felt toward her. Of course, he felt some sort of affection; that she knew. But their differences in station had always hung before her eyes like a thick curtain. She was foolish to love this man.

She gave a rueful laugh. She supposed Mrs. Whiston had been right all along—she really was a stupid girl.

"Do you really think it's true?" Elsie whispered, thinking of her mother again.

"What?" Andrew's voice rumbled through his chest.

"Do you really think she's going to live with me here in the cottage and that everything will be all right."

"I promise," said Andrew. "You and your mother are going to live here and be happy together."

Elsie squeezed her eyes tight shut. His words made it a little easier to think that a better future was real—but there was one thing that she wished she could tell him.

That more than anything, she wished he could live with them in the cottage, too.

CHAPTER 19

There was no need for Mrs. Whiston to ring the bell at night anymore. For the past few nights, Elsie had been sleeping on the rug beside the old lady's bed, alert to her every stirring through the night – and there were many. Mrs. Whiston slept fitfully, now giving a brief cough, then kicking irritably at her covers and shouting for water, then falling asleep again only to start the cycle once more.

Elsie felt as though she had just fallen asleep when she was jerked to wakefulness by a hand dangling from the bed and clutching the sleeve of her dress. Startled, Elsie sat up, blinking the sleepiness from her eyes. She felt a flash of irritation at the tightness with which Mrs. Whiston was clinging to her sleeve, but when she heard the old lady's breathing, fear shot through her.

Every breath was a rattling, labored gasp, and when Elsie scrambled up and looked down at her charge, Mrs. Whiston's eyes were wide and staring with fear. They rolled to gaze up at Elsie with a mute plea for help. Mrs. Whiston sucked in another breath, sounding like the action was draining her strength.

"Mrs. Whiston!" Elsie fell to her knees, grabbing the old lady's hand. "What's the matter? What can I do?"

Mrs. Whiston closed her eyes as she dragged in another breath, then opened them wide, trying to control the terror that threatened to overwhelm her face. "Doc… doc…" she wheezed.

Elsie stared at her for a second. Then she rushed to her feet, running to the doorway.

"Andrew!" she cried, knowing that he was asleep in the chambers just down the hall and not caring who heard her shouting his first name right now. How grateful she was that he'd decided to spend a few days with his grandmother that week since she was so poorly. "Andrew, wake up!"

There was a crash from one of the rooms down the hallway and Andrew stumbled out, his dressing-gown dangling over his frame, his hair on end. "What is it?" he spluttered.

"Mrs. Whiston." Elsie's voice shook.

In what seemed to be two long strides, Andrew was inside the room. He bent over Mrs. Whiston, laying a hand on her

A DAUGHTER'S DESPERATION

forehead. "It's all right, Granny," he said softly. "Try to be calm."

"What are we going to do?" Elsie's hands were shaking as she brushed some of Mrs. Whiston's hair out of her face.

"Send for my sisters," said Andrew shortly.

"And the doctor?"

They exchanged glances, and in that moment, Elsie knew it was likely too late for such things.

"Yes," said Andrew quietly. "Him, too."

Elsie ran down the stairs as fast as she could, shouting for the page-boy. She had to hammer on his door in the servants' quarters to rouse him, then bundled him off outside with a slip of paper in his hand as quickly as she could: *Mrs. Whiston not well. Come quickly.*

Watching the boy hurry off down the street, Elsie didn't know what to feel. She stared after him for a long moment, clutching her shawl around her. It felt as though the foundations of her world were trembling.

But there was work to do, so she didn't tarry there for long. Taking the stairs two at a time on her aching feet, Elsie hurried back up to Mrs. Whiston's chamber. She could hear the old lady's rasping even before she went into the room. Andrew was kneeling beside the bed, gently stroking his grandmother's hands, talking soothingly to her.

"Don't say such things right now, Granny," he was saying as Elsie came in. "Just try to rest. The doctor is on his way, and so are Agatha and Sophronia."

Mrs. Whiston's blue lips pressed into a bitter line. She gave a little shake of her head, then gripped the front of Andrew's shirt with terrified strength. Andrew allowed himself to be pulled closer, and Elsie heard her groaning something into his ear. A look of surprise crossed his face, and Andrew glanced up at Elsie with wide eyes.

"What is it?" Elsie asked.

Then, Mrs. Whiston coughed. The sound was wet and retching, and the old lady's face blanched ash-gray. Elsie rushed to help Andrew roll her over onto her side, and a gout of ugly pink foam dripped from Mrs. Whiston's shriveled mouth.

"Andrew." Elsie's heart was hammering with fear. "What's happening?"

"Shhh." Andrew wasn't talking to her. He grabbed a flannel from the basin by the bed and wiped his grandmother's mouth, then gently rolled her onto her back, stroking the hair away from her face. "It's all right, Granny. Just try to relax."

Mrs. Whiston's breath sounded like a cold wind between gravestones. She extended her gnarled hands toward Andrew, and he gripped them tightly.

"Hush," he said soothingly. "Hush now, Granny." The panic gradually left her eyes, and they started to close. She made a

A DAUGHTER'S DESPERATION

wet sound as if trying to clear her throat, and then murmured something.

"Sorry, Granny?" Andrew bent down to listen to her.

Mrs. Whiston tried again. "Els... Elsie," she groaned.

Elsie had never heard Mrs. Whiston use her name at all. She stood shocked, rooted to the spot, as Andrew glanced up at her. "Come on," he said gently, grabbing her arm and pulling her closer. She fell to her knees beside the bed.

"Yes, ma'am?" she whispered.

Mrs. Whiston's hand gripped her collar with surprising strength. "Never..." She sucked in another breath. "Never... become... like me." Then the hand slackened on Elsie's collar, the old lady's eyes closed, and her head lolled on the pillow.

"Is she...?" Elsie couldn't finish the sentence.

Andrew gently pressed his fingertips to Mrs. Whiston's neck. "Sleeping," he said quietly. "But... I'm afraid..."

Elsie knew the old woman didn't have long. She could hear a clattering of footsteps in the hallway and realized that she was kneeling by Mrs. Whiston's bed with Andrew's arm around her shoulders.

"I'm scared," she whispered.

Andrew pulled her closer, pressing his lips to the top of her head. "Don't be," he murmured.

They pulled apart just before Agatha and Sophronia burst into the room, both looking red-faced with the effort of running up the stairs.

"Granny!" thundered Agatha. "Granny, wake up!"

"Shhh," Andrew scolded. "She's resting. Don't wake her. She's in pain."

Sophronia ignored him flatly. Pushing him and Elsie out of the way, she wriggled to Mrs. Whiston's bedside and seized the old lady's hand in her own gigantic paw. "Granny!" she wailed. "Oh, Granny, Granny!"

Mrs. Whiston's eyes snapped open. She fixed Sophronia with a furious glare.

"I'm not... dead yet..." she rasped.

Both sisters seemed slightly taken aback by this turn of events. They hesitated for a second, and in that pause, a tall man with long white whiskers bustled into the room. Elsie recognized him as Mrs. Whiston's physician, Dr. King.

"Doctor," beseeched Sophronia shrilly, turning to him.

"Oh, at last, a doctor," cried Agatha. "Please, good sir, I beg of you." She simpered, giving him a gummy smile. "Heal my grandmother. She means the world to us all."

Dr. King gave them both a severe look. "I'm well aware of what she means to you two," he said. "Now, get out of this room, unless you are going to compose yourselves and sit

A DAUGHTER'S DESPERATION

quietly. Your grandmother is very ill." He glanced down at the lump of pink foam lying on the floor beside the bed. "Very ill indeed. She needs peace and quiet around her right now."

Suitably chastised, the two sisters heaved themselves into chairs by the bed while Dr. King bent down to examine Mrs. Whiston. His expression told Elsie everything that she needed to know: that this, indeed, was the final hour. She inched closer until she could get hold of Mrs. Whiston's hand, interlacing the limp and arthritic fingers in her own.

It was simply a bid to do what she felt was right, even with Andrew and the sisters staring. Elsie felt that someone should hold the woman's hand. And who better to do so than the girl who'd been caring for Mrs. Whiston for the past five years?

Perhaps the old lady did appreciate it a little. Her eyes fluttered open, and she stared at Elsie for a few seconds. Something that might have been contentment—or perhaps it was just relief, spread across her face. Then the woman's chest gave a strange little heave, and her eyes grew glassy, staring at Elsie with an emptiness that chilled her to the very marrow of her bones.

"Dr. King?" Elsie gasped.

Dr. King bent down and gently touched Mrs. Whiston's neck. With a respectful motion, he softly closed her eyes for the last time. "I'm afraid she's gone," he said.

"NO!" Agatha's dramatic scream made Elsie startle so badly

that she leapt to her feet. Mrs. Whiston's hand slipped out of hers, flopping lifelessly back onto the bed.

"Not now, Agatha," snapped Andrew.

"Noooo!" Agatha wailed again, grasping at her scarf as if to tear it. "Granny! Grannyyyy!"

"Now, now, dear." Alarmed, Dr. King reached for Agatha's arm. "Compose yourself. This won't do, you know."

Sophronia gave a little sigh and crumpled to the floor. Andrew rolled his eyes visibly.

"Would you two stop?" he begged. "Do you have no respect for our grandmother's memory?"

Elsie felt lost, detached somehow, like a tugboat floating around in a bay that had just been vacated by the ship that it was used to attending. She sat down slowly on the chair beside Mrs. Whiston's body. When her arm brushed against her mistress's leg, it was still warm, almost as if she might sit up and start complaining about her tea at any moment.

Agatha spotted Elsie, and her face blanched with rage. She raised an enormous finger and jabbed it accusingly at her. "YOU!" she bellowed.

Elsie started at her.

"YOU! You were supposed to care for our grandmother," Agatha roared. "Now look at her. Look at her! She's dead!"

A DAUGHTER'S DESPERATION

"I can assure you that Mrs. Whiston's passing is more due to old age than anything else," said Dr. King briskly, giving Elsie a sympathetic glance.

"I want her out," Agatha said, her voice steel. "Get her out!"

"No."

The word was spoken with such a flat, final quality that it brought sudden and abrupt silence to the entire room. Even Sophronia sat up, her expression as guilty as that of a child caught in mischief. Andrew stepped forward, protectively placing himself between Elsie and Agatha. "Elsie's not going anywhere," he said firmly. "She was closer to Grandmother than any of us."

"Face it, Andrew," Agatha said. "Your little pet maid has no more use now that Grandmother's dead." Her former faux grief had given way to icy rationalism. "She needs to go."

"No, she doesn't," said Andrew. "You've forgotten that she owns the cottage in the orchard now. She has as much a right to be here as you and I do."

Agatha's eyes narrowed. "That's if Grandmother still kept to that ridiculous clause in her will," she snapped. "She might have changed it. You wouldn't know."

"That's as may be," said Andrew, "but neither would you know. Right now, you have no right to order Elsie to go anywhere – not until the will has been read, at any rate."

Agatha's face went from white to scarlet. Her fists bunched at her sides, but she knew as well as Andrew did that he was right.

"Fine," she whispered icily. "But the moment that the will reveals – and *it will reveal* – that that little piece of street filth has inherited nothing from our esteemed grandmother's estate, I want her gone." Her arms folded. "Gone forever."

Elsie had had enough. She rose to her feet, giving Mrs. Whiston's body a final glance. She walked out of the room, her back as stiff as a ramrod. And she only allowed herself to cry when she'd reached her quarters – and when she did, she felt as though the tears would never, ever stop.

CHAPTER 20

It didn't rain on the day of Mrs. Whiston's funeral. Instead, the sun was shining, birds sang in the trees—the perfect wintry air diamond-still and ice-cold as the Whiston carriage clopped back toward the manor. It was Elsie's first time in the carriage, but as she leaned against the velvet cushions and watched the streets skimming past through the window, she didn't feel excited.

After crying all morning, she was surprised to find that she didn't feel anything much anymore. She supposed she should be worried about the reading of the will, which was to take place in the manor as soon as they returned; or saddened about Mrs. Whiston's death, considering that grief had been overwhelming her all day. Or perhaps even a little relieved that the old tyrant had shuffled off the mortal coil at last.

Instead, all she felt was numbness and exhaustion. She was also exceedingly uncomfortable in the family carriage where Andrew had insisted she ride.

"Are you all right?" Andrew asked. He sat beside her, his hands resting in his lap, but his body close enough that she could feel his warmth.

Sitting opposite them, the two sisters gave both Andrew and Elsie a death glare. Elsie tried to ignore them, smiling weakly at Andrew. "I'm quite all right, thank you," she said.

Andrew cleared his throat. "It's been a long day," he said gently.

The carriage jolted as they came to a halt in front of the manor house. Footmen opened the doors, and Agatha and Sophronia descended first, shooting angry glances at Andrew as he followed and held out a hand to help Elsie down from the carriage. Elsie was acutely aware that he was breaking convention – at least, he was right now.

In a few minutes, the solicitor would read out Mrs. Whiston's will and prove that Elsie was the legal owner of the cottage, and then the two sisters wouldn't be able to say a thing. She would go home, Elsie decided, to the tenement and get Mama ready straight away. Perhaps Andrew would help her by hailing a cab for her – she would be a land-owning lady then, so it wouldn't be unseemly for them to be seen together anymore.

But it hadn't happened yet, and so once Elsie's feet were on the paving of the driveway, Andrew dropped his hand to his side with an apologetic smile. Agatha led them all into the parlor. Elsie almost stoked the fire herself out of sheer habit, but the parlor-maid had already seen to it, and the solicitor was warming himself by the hearth when they all came in.

"Good afternoon," he said. He was a portly figure with a wig that was a little too long for him, and his words were as round and pompous as the curls on the end of that wig. "I regret to hear about the passing of Mrs. Agnes Whiston."

His words were emotionless. Elsie and the siblings nodded mutely.

"Let's get to it, then," said the solicitor. "Why don't you all take a seat?"

Andrew sank into a chair, while the two sisters took the settee. Awkwardly, Elsie hovered. She couldn't fathom sitting down in Mrs. Whiston's old armchair; just looking at it made her skin crawl a little, remembering the thousands of hours that the old lady had spent reading, napping, visiting and complaining in it.

"Very well." The solicitor sniffed and took out a tremendous document, penned in an elegant hand, finished off at the bottom with a shining red seal that Elsie recognized as the same mark that was on the doors of the carriages.

"*This is the Last Will and Testament of me, Agnes Magnolia Whis-*

ton," he read aloud, *"of Whiston Manor, End Street, Piccadilly. I hereby bequeath my many and wonderful possessions to my surviving relatives as follows: To my twin granddaughters, the Misses Agatha and Sophronia Whiston, I bequeath my manor house, the grounds, and all of its contents, including the livestock, the carriages, the priceless heirlooms within the house, the elaborate furnishings and the unique works of art hanging on the walls and displayed in all the hallways."*

The solicitor took a deep breath and wiped his forehead with his handkerchief, as if a little worn out by the long sentence. *"This includes the manor grounds, with the exception of the cottage located in the back of the orchard on the eastern side of the manor house."*

Elsie's heart was beating very fast. She realized that she was wringing her own handkerchief in her hands, and that they were shaking. This was it. The moment her life was going to change forever.

"The cottage I bequeath," the solicitor read, *"to my dear grandson, Mr. Andrew Whiston, for him to dwell in with his lady wife."*

"What?"

It took Elsie a second to realize that she had spoken. The siblings all turned to stare at her; the siblings with sneers of triumph, Andrew with an expression of shock.

"You have the cottage?" Elsie gasped, staring at Andrew. She was out of place to speak at all, but she couldn't stop the words. She should have known. She had her place in society just as Andrew had his. She had been a complete fool to think such things could change.

"Elsie—" Andrew began.

Elsie's entire body was trembling. She felt horribly betrayed. "No," she said, backing away. "No, don't say anything."

Andrew rose. "I can explain," he began.

Elsie held out a hand, her face burning with shame. "No," she said, turning toward the door.

"Elsie," Andrew tried again. "Elsie, wait!"

But Elsie was already running back down the hallways, bolting out of the front door, pelting across the manor grounds as fast as her legs could carry her, then heading into the vast streets of London, hoping that some part of its deep and pockmarked heart would swallow her whole and make her disappear forever.

ELSIE'S SHOES AND FEET WERE TORN WHEN SHE REACHED the tenement building. She had another pair of shoes, back at the manor, lying in her old quarters with her blanket and spare dress, but Elsie couldn't care less. She stumbled into the tenement, wanting nothing in the world except for her mother's warm embrace.

But when the door swung open, Elsie felt chilled to the bone. Mama lay on the sleeping mat, her eyes closed, and her face wasn't just gray today. She looked ... blue.

"Mama?" The word came out as a croak through a throat that was worn from weeping.

For one, long, terrible moment, nothing happened. Then Mama's eyes fluttered opened, and an attempt at a smile tugged at her lips.

"Elsie," she whispered, the word a dried-up leaf skittering on the edge of hearing. The blanket fell away as she extended two arms that resembled dry sticks.

Elsie ran to her, and carefully lay beside her. Mama held her with surprising vigor, the strength of her love utterly unabated by the illness that had wrought havoc throughout her body. She kissed Elsie's forehead, stroked her hair, murmured words of reassurance as Elsie wept inconsolably into her mother's breast.

"What happened, my love?" Mama whispered. Each word seemed to be an effort. "What's the matter?"

"We didn't get the cottage, Mama," Elsie choked out. "Mrs. Whiston is dead, and we didn't get the cottage. We don't have anything now, Mama. We don't have a thing. I don't have a position, we don't have a house, and I don't know how we're going to – how I could possibly—"

She choked a little, hiccupping in her grief. "I don't know how we're going to pay the rent. Or eat. And – and it was Andrew." A hot new rush of tears poured down her cheeks. "Andrew took the cottage from us. Andrew betrayed me, and I thought he was my friend." More quietly, almost to herself, she murmured, "I thought he was more than a friend."

"Oh, Elsie." Mama's hands were trembling with weakness, but she still used them to cup Elsie's face and tip it up so that she could gaze into her eyes. "Did you speak with him?"

"No," Elsie whispered.

"Why not?"

"Because he betrayed us, Mama. He took it all from us."

"My darling," Mama whispered, "no cottage will ever be more important than love."

"I didn't say that I loved him," Elsie answered.

There was no response from Mama. Her eyes were closed; her breathing fluttered, and Elsie thought that maybe she had fallen asleep. Elsie laid a hand on her cheek and felt its fevered warmth, and she felt a tide of exhaustion unlike anything she'd ever known swamp her.

How was she going to do this? How was she going to survive after losing Mama, too? She knew that her mother was dying. It was shocking that she'd lasted all these years. It was only a matter of time, and then she would be completely and utterly alone.

"I don't know what to do, Mama," she whispered, gathering her mother's withered form into her arms and rocking her gently, resting her head on top of Mama's. "I just don't know what to do."

Mama stirred, one hand reaching up to clasp the back of Elsie's neck. "Rest, child," she murmured. "Just rest."

※

The next morning, Mama died in Elsie's arms. And Elsie did not have a soul left in all the great, empty, icy world.

CHAPTER 21

One Year Later

ANDREW'S ARMS WERE WARM AND STRONG. THEY ENCIRCLED Elsie's waist with a thoughtless grace, spinning and moving her this way and that in the warm kitchen, their feet moving seamlessly together in perfect time to the cheerful music of the fiddle that had filled the little room from one edge to the other. Elsie laughed, shaking back her torrent of shiny dark hair, gazing up into Andrew's eyes. They were dancing, too, just as quick and vibrant as the rhythm of their feet upon the floor. The air was filled with the smells of the meal that was cooking on the stove, and Elsie still had a wooden spoon clutched in the hand that rested on Andrew's shoulder, but she didn't care. She was safe and warm, and all was well.

The song came to an end, and Elsie looked up, still laughing and a *little dizzy. A boy stood by the kitchen table, his fiddle still on his shoulder. He had Andrew's eyes. "Again, Mama, again!" he laughed, twirling the bow.*

"Leave your poor mother alone! She's got to get your supper cooked," another voice spoke playfully. Elsie turned, and there she was, standing in the doorway, whole and healthy. Her cheeks glowed rosily, her eyes bright and shining with joy.

"Mama!" Elsie cried. She pulled away from Andrew, reaching out her arms, running toward her mother. "Mama, you're here!"

She threw out her arms to embrace her. But they met with nothingness, her fingers groping at empty air. Spinning around, Elsie felt fear rush through her body. The whole, happy Mama was gone; instead she lay on the floor, the floor of the tenement, her eyes staring, her body skeletal and shriveled. Elsie stared at her, mute and confused. Then two men pushed through the doorway, roughly shoving her. They grabbed Mama's arms and legs, hoisting her like she was nothing.

"No!" Elsie rushed at them, grabbing their arms. "No! Don't take her! NO!"

Elsie sat up, gasping. Sweat was running down her face; she knew from the echoes in the room that her own screams had woken her once again. She looked around wildly, but the tenement was empty. Just as it had been every single morning since that dreadful day when the undertakers had come to cart Mama away – a scene that replayed in her dreams almost every night.

"Oh, Mama." Elsie squeezed her eyes tightly shut against the tide of grief that threatened to overwhelm her. She hugged her knees to her chest and coughed, choking a bit on the mucous, her muscles aching with the illness that had been gripping her for weeks.

"I miss you," she whispered through a hoarse, raw throat.

The tenement was cold, but there was no time to make a fire. Elsie knew that she had to be at work soon, despite the fact that every muscle in her body ached. She dragged herself to her feet, feeling more beaten than she'd ever been in her life. Another coughing fit froze her to the spot, forcing her to ride it out. She bent double with the force of it. Her entire body was trembling when it was finally over.

There was no breakfast, no warm water to wash in, so Elsie just raked her hair back into something of a braid and then stumbled out of the tenement. The low, gray clouds threatened snow; their chill sucked at her sore joints as she stumbled along the streets, heading deeper and deeper into the slums. The walk was barely enough to warm her; in a few minutes, she could see the stern, squat shape of the factory building up ahead.

A tide of women joined Elsie in shuffling through the doorway of the factory and into its clanking, noisy belly. She remembered how the towering machines all around her had always frightened her. She'd hated the way they moved and thumped over one another, a fact made even worse when she'd seen what the machines could do to the hapless little children who were forced to work underneath them, sweeping them and keeping them oiled. But now, she could think of nothing except the way that her lungs burned and how heavy her eyelids were. She staggered over to the bench where she worked. Already, a sheet of rough fabric was lying there, ready to be sewn into a cheap sheet.

Elsie stood there, staring at it, for a long moment. She didn't want to pick up her spool of hairy thread and the big, blunt needle. Her hands were calloused and aching already, and she hadn't even started her twelve-hour day yet. But she had no choice. She had to eat. Slowly, stiffly, she threaded the needle and got to work.

Hour after hour trickled by. Women stood on either side of Elsie, but she barely knew their faces, let alone their names; looking up or talking to each other would get you fined or beaten by one of the overseers who stalked up and down the rows of benches. Her eyelids drooped, her hands cramped, and every breath made her lungs burn. She swallowed hard, trying to keep from coughing too much. If she ruined a sheet, she would be beaten for sure.

It was long past their ten-minute lunch break, and Elsie was starting to think that the day would last forever, when it happened. The needle slipped. Elsie felt a brief stab of pain. Sluggish with exhaustion, she could only stare as a huge drop of blood welled up on the tip of her finger. Before she could do anything, it fell, tumbling slowly through the air. *Splat*. The blood landed in the center of the sheet, and the red stain spread in all directions, seeping into the fabric.

Elsie froze. Her heart was beating wildly, erratically, but she couldn't persuade her limbs to move.

"Oi!" An angry voice rose up behind her. "You! What are you doing?"

Elsie turned, hanging her head automatically. She knew better than to say anything. Nothing could stop what was coming, and she stared down at the overseer's feet. He stomped to a halt in front of her, and his voice dripped with disdain. "Look at what you've done!" He seized the sheet, raising it under her nose. "This is ruined. Destroyed!" Throwing it carelessly aside, the overseer reached for his belt. "That's going to cost you dearly," he snarled.

"Wait." Another voice spoke, and Elsie looked up, wondering if she could dare to hope. One of the factory managers stood beside the overseer, and the expression on his face quickly killed any hope she'd had. He looked at her sneeringly, his thin mustache twisting. "It's no good, Higgins," he told the overseer. "If you lay a finger on this one, she'll drop dead."

"So what do you want me to do?" the overseer demanded.

"Nothing." The manager gave Elsie a dismissive flick of the hand. "You're no good for work in this state. You're fired."

"What?" His words were a bucket of ice water down Elsie's

back. "No! Sir, please. I've just got a little cold. Please, sir. Please, I need this—"

"Go before I set the dogs on you," the factory manager snapped. "Higgins, go into the streets and find me a replacement at once. Take this one with you – and make sure she doesn't come back."

Higgins reached for Elsie's arm, but she shrank back. "I'm going," she said meekly. "I'm going."

The next thing she knew, she was staggering out onto the streets. A thin sleet had begun to fall. The busy street was packed with people hurrying to and fro, bundled up from top to bottom against the icy wind. It hissed thinly around Elsie's neck and bare ankles, making her shiver. She wrapped her arms around herself, feeling a terrible bleakness fill her heart. What was she going to do now? Where could she go? She would be evicted from her latest tenement in a few days. She had nothing to eat for supper.

"Oh, Mama." Elsie closed her eyes, sighing. "I wish you were here to tell me what to do right now."

A memory drifted to the front of her mind, gently nudging her with its warmth. She sat down on the pavement and allowed it to fill her. The night she'd learned that Andrew had betrayed her and taken the cottage. Coming home and crying in Mama's arms. And Mama's words then, soothing a pain as raw and real as it still was right now: *My darling, no cottage will ever be more important than love.*

A DAUGHTER'S DESPERATION

Elsie remembered the way Andrew had spoken to her. The way that he touched her. The love in his eyes. A surge of desperation ran through her, and she struggled to remain on her feet. She had nothing left to lose now. She would go to him and beg. Maybe, he would have pity on her.

Or maybe he wouldn't recognize her. She knew she was only a shell of who she used to be. Hunger and sickness gnawed at her. Maybe she should just lie down and let God take her. She was near death—that she knew. Would she join her mother then? And her father?

The thought warmed her heart for a brief second, but then the cold of the air pierced through her thin clothing again. She'd done her best. She'd always done her best. But now, there was nothing left she could do. Nothing.

Except beg. Her face screwed up in a pained expression. *No.* Not beg. Just ask. She could ask for help. She *would ask Andrew.* And she would pay him back. Yes. She always paid her way.

Her thinking grew fuzzy, and she wasn't sure exactly where she was anymore. She stumbled on down the street. Whiston Manor. Whiston Manor. She grabbed passersby to ask directions, but they shook her off, clearly offended and even frightened. She nearly lost her balance more than once.

"Whiston Manor," she muttered as loudly as she could. Finally, someone pointed. She kept walking, her mind clearing enough now so she knew she was headed in the right direction.

Keep going, she urged herself. *Keep going. Keep going. Keep going.*

TO ELSIE'S SURPRISE, NOBODY STOPPED HER FROM WALKING down the driveway of Whiston Manor. The sleet was falling faster now, leaving the pavement slick and wet. Elsie had to tread carefully, and it was just as well. She couldn't bear to look up at the manor house, knowing that Agatha and Sophronia were sitting in those warm rooms, complaining and fighting just as Mrs. Whiston had always done, probably abusing the servants that had remained, even though Elsie was gone.

Instead, she trudged straight past it, determined not to be distracted from her goal.

Ask. Ask. Ask him. That was all she would do.

The orchard was bare, its trees leafless in the winter cold, the shape of their branches sketched with brutal clarity against the gray sky; Elsie glanced up into the familiar tree. Her robin wasn't there. She faltered along the footpath until she rounded the bend and there it was – the cottage. *Her* cottage. Except now, it was more than just an empty shell waiting to be filled by her dreams. Candlelight glowed in the windows, pooling warmly on the cold earth in front of the cottage;

wood smoke rose from the chimney, and she could smell something cooking.

Tears filled her eyes. Her throat tightened. She coughed.

Tentatively, she took a few steps nearer. Andrew was sitting inside at the kitchen table. She could see him clearly through the window. His hair was messy; he wore a shirt that was half unbuttoned, and he was bent over a piece of paper on the table, his lips pursed with concentration as he wrote. For a few moments, Elsie could do nothing but stare at him. Her vision blurred, and she knew she was crying.

The sight of him was like a physical blow. She hadn't realized how much she had missed the shade of his eyes, the slant of his mouth, the perfect unity of his eyebrows as he frowned in deep focus. Suddenly, all she wanted to do was collapse in his arms. It was too much. Seeing him was *too much*.

It didn't matter that he was sitting in the cottage that should have been rightfully hers. Nothing mattered – nothing except her need to be near him again.

She started forward. And then she saw *her*. The woman standing by the stove, an apron tied in a neat little bow at her waist. She was young and slim, and when she turned around, Elsie saw how pretty she was, and the sight was a knife straight through her heart.

"No!" Elsie cried, her voice scratchy and terrified. "No! It can't be!"

They both looked up at her cry. Andrew, the man she should have had, the man she loved – and his new wife.

Elsie couldn't face it, couldn't bear it. Her last ray of hope shattered into a thousand fragments, that the wind now blew away, scattering the pieces she would never find again. She turned and ran, ignoring her aching limps, pushing aside her pounding heart and burning lungs. All she knew was that she had to run. She had to get away.

She had to find an escape from her utterly broken heart.

CHAPTER 22

The world was spinning around Elsie, and she hardly knew which way to run. So she just stood, nearly falling, on the street corner, her skirts clutched in both hands, her chest heaving with effort. All around her, traffic whirled past: schoolchildren ran down the pavement, men hurried and brushed against her as they passed, carriages charged up and down the street, and in the center of it all, feeling as if the very earth was spinning beneath her feet, was Elsie.

How could this have happened? How had the bottom been ripped out of her world so thoroughly, so brutally, in one single year? She didn't want to close her eyes in case she saw the triumph on Agatha's and Sophronia's faces, or the weakness of her mother's final moments, or – perhaps worst of them all – Andrew and his new wife working together in the kitchen. She knew that there were tears streaming down her cheeks, that she was coughing and gasping uncontrollably, and that passers-by were staring at her. She didn't care. What was left in her world? Who was left that cared at all about whether she, Elsie Griggs, lived or died?

She felt she might die right here. She was so dizzy that it felt as if her spirit were clinging onto her body by a mere thread, and that at any moment, that thread would snap, and she would float away to some kinder place. Her knees trembled, threatening to buckle. Would anyone care if she fell down right here, right now?

She took a deep breath, trying to steady herself, but it only sent her into a paroxysm of coughs. In her whirling mind, she clutched at a happy memory. *Andrew*. Andrew was in her happy memories, but had he ever really cared for her? Had he ever said a genuinely kind word to her, or had there been some hidden motive all along? She allowed her eyes to flutter closed, even though that made her knees feel wobbly. She had always loved the way that he'd said her name. *Elsie*. He said it like it was something precious, rolling it around on his tongue like a pearl in the mouth of an oyster. *Elsie. Elsie.*

"Elsie?"

Her eyes flew open. He was standing there, a few yards away, directly in front of her. For a moment she thought that perhaps she was dreaming again, but the smell of the street and the sweat on his brow was real.

She wanted to holler at him. She wanted to slap him. She wanted to hug him. Instead, she forced her voice to speak. "Andrew," she eked out. "What do you want?"

"Elsie." Andrew's eyes were limpid with emotion. He took a step nearer, reaching a hand toward her, but when she shrank back, he allowed it to fall down by his side again. "I can't believe I've finally found you."

"Finally found me?" Elsie shook her head. "I came to find *you*."

"I've been searching, Elsie." Andrew's voice was low, urgent. "Oh, dear God, I've been searching for you ever since you ran out of that manor house the day my grandmother's will was read. I even hired people to look for you."

"I had to change tenements more than once. But why? Why look for me?" Elsie asked, her mind clouding again. Her voice came out as a quavering whisper. "You ... got what you wanted. The cottage..."

"Why would I care about the cottage? Oh, Elsie." Andrew took another step closer. "All I've ever wanted is you."

"But your ... your wife?"

"Wife?" Andrew looked puzzled for a moment.

"The woman in your cottage with you."

"What, you mean Miriam?" Pity and relief spread over Andrew's face. "Elsie, she's my housemaid. Nothing more."

"H-housemaid?" said Elsie faintly.

"Yes. Yes, of course, Elsie." His eyes misted over. "You're all that I've ever wanted," he whispered huskily. "I've never wanted anything else except for you."

The warmth of his voice was a homecoming, a lifeline to Elsie as she fought to remain standing. He *wanted her?* Was her mind playing tricks again? She ... she should go to him. But as she stepped forward, her failing body gave out at last. Her knees crumpled beneath her. The last thing she knew was his arms surrounding her as darkness closed over her mind.

☙❧

SOMETHING COOL WAS PATTING ELSIE'S FOREHEAD. SHE tried to raise a hand to brush it away, irritated, a frown tugging at her brow. The sensation was pleasant on her warm skin, but she wanted to sleep, to sink back into the warm darkness and sleep away the pain that was seeping through her muscles. Her limbs all ached; her lungs ached even more, but she was lying on something inexpressibly soft and warm, the most comfortable surface she'd ever lain on. Her head was pillowed on what felt like a piece of cloud, and there was cool linen against her skin, so light and soft that it felt like little more than air.

But the patting continued on her face, cleansing burning sweat from her skin. She gave a groan that made her throat sting and tried to raise a hand again, but all that she could manage was a twitch of her fingers.

"Shhh." The voice was familiar, and so lovely that Elsie lay still, wanting simply to listen to it. "It's all right, Elsie. Don't try to move. Just rest, my dear. Just rest."

Andrew? Elsie's eyes fluttered open. He was leaning over her, dabbing at her face with a damp cloth, wearing shirtsleeves; there were dark circles underneath his eyes, but his smile was real. "Hello there," he said softly, lowering the cloth and laying his hand on the side of her face instead.

Elsie relaxed, gazing up at him. "What's h-happening?" she whispered.

"You've been sick," said Andrew. "Very, very sick. I was…" He took a deep breath, letting it out slowly. "I was worried about you. But your fever is breaking now. You'll be all right." He tried to smile. "I qualified as a doctor since you left, you know."

The way he said *you know* reminded her of Mrs. Whiston, but not in a bad way. She tried to smile. "Where am I?"

"In the cottage. *Your* cottage, Elsie."

"It's not mine," Elsie croaked. "It's yours." She blinked at him. "Why did you bring me here?"

"Well, my sisters sold the manor house to strangers." Andrew shrugged. "And this is home now, so there was nowhere much else to go."

Elsie frowned. "H-home?" she whispered.

"Let me show you something." Andrew leaned forward to kiss her forehead, then stepped away from the bed. Elsie felt his kiss burning on her forehead like a living thing. She gazed around the room as Andrew vanished. It was one of the smaller bedrooms that she'd always pictured giving to her children, but instead of empty and dirty, it was neatly decorated and warmed by lamplight.

"Here." Andrew sat down on a chair beside the bed again. He was holding a handwritten note.

"What's that?" asked Elsie.

"A note from my grandmother," said Andrew. "Dated the day that she died."

"That's not her hand," said Elsie. "She couldn't write in her last days, either."

"I know. I believe it's in Mrs. Corbyn's handwriting," said Andrew. "I suppose my grandmother dictated this to her – it seems she was too stubborn to say it to you directly, but she had to say it to someone. She left this in a box of her personal things, and I found it only a few days after her funeral."

Elsie struggled to sit up. The effort made her feel flushed, but

A DAUGHTER'S DESPERATION

Andrew quickly helped her, putting some more pillows behind her back. She shook a sweaty lock of hair out of her face. "What does it say?"

Andrew smiled. "I'll read it to you," he said. "It's addressed to me, but I know it's meant for you, too."

"But why would your grandmother leave me a note? And on her deathbed?"

"Just listen." Andrew cleared his throat. "*My dearest grandson, Andrew Whiston. I am well aware that I have come to my final hours, and that the time has come for me to meet my Maker. I have always considered myself a most educated and accomplished woman, as you know. Noble blood runs through my veins, and I have done it great justice with the way in which I lived my life.*

"*However, now that I find myself at the end of my life, I realize that I am completely alone. In fact, for most of my life, I was completely alone — even when your grandfather was alive.*"

Elsie listened mutely, having no idea of Mrs. Whiston's sentiments.

"*For whatever reason, in my twilight hours, I have been left with practically nothing,*" Andrew read on. "*My earthly affairs are in order. My house is in the most pristine condition, and I have taken great care for all of the treasures within. Yet now, it matters little to me. I am completely alone, with not a heart in the world that cares for me — except for my little personal maid, Elsie Griggs.*"

"What?" whispered Elsie.

"She knew that you cared for her, Elsie." Andrew reached over and interlaced his fingers with hers. His touch was warm, perfect. "Listen to this. *Elsie has served me with great faithfulness over the years. She has been the only source of love in my life ever since she came into it, and I wish for her – and for you – to experience that same love. I strongly desire for you both to know love before you are old and tired on your deathbeds. For that reason, I am making a small change to my will.*"

Andrew glanced up at Elsie, nervous excitement tugging his mouth into that crooked smile. "*I am leaving the cottage to you, Andrew, so those wretched sisters of you won't fight my will. Now marry Elsie Griggs, as I know you have been in love with her for years. Experience the simple joy and love that I never permitted for myself. Live the life that I withheld from myself. I trust you and Elsie will have very many happy years in the cottage together. And Andrew, if you don't marry the girl, you're a fool. And if that's the case, give the cottage to her like I promised. Your grandmother, Mrs. Agnes Magnolia Whiston.*"

Elsie realized that tears were running freely down her cheeks. She didn't say anything; she didn't think she could speak.

Andrew looked up at her, his eyes dancing. "So you see, Elsie?" he said softly. "She didn't leave the cottage to me. She left it to both of us."

"Her ... last words." Elsie had to swallow hard before she could finish her sentence. "Her last words to me were, 'Never become like me'. She was lonely, Andrew." She gave a small sob. "She was a sad person."

"She was." Andrew smiled, reaching up to wipe away Elsie's tears.

"My-my mother died," Elsie whispered.

"Oh, Elsie, I've often wondered. I'm so sorry."

"Right after your grandmother..."

"Elsie. I'm sorry."

"She ... she never got to know you."

"Nor I her," Andrew said. "I believe I would have loved her very much."

Elsie's eyes filled with tears yet again. "She would have loved you," she choked out.

Andrew squeezed her hand. "I didn't always do what my grandmother wished me to do," he said slowly.

She watched him speak, her love for him so strong, it was a living thing inside her.

"But this..." He held up the letter. "This, I want to do. Elsie, will you marry me?"

He reached out, pulling her into his arms, holding her with trembling sincerity.

"There's nothing I want more in all the world, Andrew," she said.

EPILOGUE

One Year Later

Flower petals rained down on Elsie, pelting on her silken bodice, sliding off the veil that tumbled down her long hair and threatening to tickle her face. She giggled, clinging onto Andrew's hand, and held up a hand to shield her face. Andrew was laughing beside her, a deep and happy sound that rumbled through his entire body.

"Whoever heard of throwing flower petals?" he asked, laughing, as they hurried down the church steps. Around them, their excited friends were throwing handfuls of petals into the air. Andrew's old friends from school, the new friends that Elsie had made in the past year, even Florence, who was still the cook at Whiston Manor.

"We'll avoid them," Elsie laughed breathlessly. She seized a handful of her thick white skirts. "Come on, Andrew. Run!"

Giggling, clinging to one another, they ran down the steps of the church toward the waiting carriage. A white horse stood between the shafts, plumes and flowers blossoming from its bridle; the footman who held the door for them was decked out in white livery. Elsie and Andrew tumbled into the carriage to laughter from their friends outside.

"Thank you!" Elsie cried, waving to them as Andrew pulled the door shut. "Thank you!"

Then, the carriage began to move. Andrew sat down beside her, his face red with laughter. Still breathless, he reached over to pick a petal out of Elsie's hair. His eyes lingered on hers, and the crooked smile filled his face. "You look happy, my beautiful bride," he murmured.

"How could I be anything but happy?" Elsie beamed up at him. "I've just gotten married to you."

Andrew leaned in and gave her a gentle kiss, his lips caressing hers in a way that made her hearth thunder. Pulling back, he gave a contented sigh. "I can't believe I was lucky enough to marry you."

Elsie gazed out of the window for a moment, thinking of everyone who had contributed to bringing her to this moment. Mama. The dear tailor, Mr. Brown. Philip, in his own way, now still stuck in Australia. Even Mrs. Whiston herself, cruel as she had always been. She looked up at Andrew, and her heart beat rapidly with gratitude.

"Me neither," she whispered. "All my dearest dreams are coming true right now."

Andrew put an arm around her shoulders. "Are you ready?" he asked.

Elsie closed her eyes for a second, considering her future. For the first time in her life, all she could see when she thought of the future was golden light. Beautiful, golden light.

"Yes," she murmured. "Yes, I'm ready."

The End

CONTINUE READING...

Thank you for reading *A Daughter's Desperation!*

Are you wondering what to read next? Why not read ***The Factory Girl's Song?*** **Here's a sneak peek for you:**

Olive knew that Father was getting worse.

She watched him as he walked across their tiny tenement, keeping her head ducked, her dirty and stringy dark hair falling over her eyes as she tried to scrub the floor. She didn't want him to know that she knew how sick he was – it would only make him and Mother worry even more.

Still, she knew by the way he moved that his entire body was aching. He didn't so much walk as drag himself, his thin frame staggering across the grubby floor. Everything about him seemed to rattle: his thin shoulders in their sockets, his

A DAUGHTER'S DESPERATION

bruised fingers against each other, his breath as it struggled in and out of a chest clogged with sickness. When he sat down, slowly, on the upturned bucket that was all they had for a chair, his frame seemed to shrink. He seemed so... defeated. Like life had given him one beating too many.

Father looked up. Olive hurriedly turned back to her work, moving the dry brush across the floor with all of her might. It was a tattered thing, its last few bristles scraping pathetically on the wooden floor, not so much removing the grime as simply raking a few scratches in it. Olive wondered how many families had stayed here in this tiny tenement, how much death and disease this little room had seen. How much of it was here on the floor, where she knelt in her ragged dress, her thin arms forcing the brush down harder and harder.

She wished she could scrub it away – all of it - the illness that had changed her strong and lively father into this skeleton of a man. The worry that had worn lines around her mother's eyes, aging her ten years in a matter of months. The way that hunger had stolen the plump cheeks of her little brother Jimmy, himself reduced to a scrawny shadow of the bouncing five-year-old he had been before the illness came for Father.

Olive knew she wasn't supposed to notice these things. She was only eight years old, after all. But she did, and the sight of them weighed on her soul.

"Olive." Her father's voice was gentle. "Why don't you stop

there? I don't think..." He paused. "I don't think there's much more you can do right now."

Olive took a deep breath and laid down the brush.

"Hello, Father," she said. It took all of her courage to smile. Sometimes the weight of their poverty felt like it was crushing her, small as she was, but she couldn't let Father see her suffer. She went over to him and laid a small hand on his bony knee. "How are you doing today?"

"Better, love." Father always gave the same answer, even as Olive watched him wasting away. "Much better."

Visit Here to Continue Reading:

http://www.ticahousepublishing.com/victorian-romance.html

THANKS FOR READING

If you **love Victorian Romance**, **Visit Here:**

https://victorian.subscribemenow.com/

to hear about all **New Faye Godwin Romance Releases! I will let you know as soon as they become available!**

Thank you, Friends! If you enjoyed *A Daughter's Desperation!* would you kindly take a couple minutes to leave a positive review on Amazon? It only takes a moment, and positive reviews truly make a difference. Thank you so much! I appreciate it!

Much love,

Faye Godwin

MORE FAYE GODWIN VICTORIAN ROMANCES!

We love rich, dramatic Victorian Romances and have a library of Faye Godwin titles just for you! (Remember that ALL of Faye's Victorian titles can be downloaded FREE with Kindle Unlimited!)

VISIT HERE to discover Faye's Complete Collection of Victorian Romance:

http://ticahousepublishing.com/victorian-romance.html

ABOUT THE AUTHOR

Faye Godwin has been fascinated with Victorian Romance since she was a teen. After reading every Victorian Romance in her public library, she decided to start writing them herself —which she's been doing ever since. Faye lives with her husband and young son in England. She loves to travel throughout her country, dreaming up new plots for her romances. She's delighted to join the Tica House Publishing family and looks forward to getting to know her readers.

contact@ticahousepublishing.com

Printed in Great Britain
by Amazon